WE
MADE A
MOViE

WE MADE A MOVIE

CHARLOTTE LO

nosy
crow

For Dad, because you never hang up the phone,
even when I've got nothing to say.
For Mum, because of the 3,744 hours of
babysitting, and the coffees.

First published in the UK in 2021 by Nosy Crow Ltd
The Crow's Nest, 14 Baden Place, Crosby Row,
London SE1 1YW, UK

Nosy Crow and associated logos are trademarks and/or registered
trademarks of Nosy Crow Ltd

Text © Charlotte Lo, 2021
Cover illustration © Aviel Basil, 2021

The right of Charlotte Lo to be identified as the author of this work
has been asserted by her in accordance with the Copyright, Designs
and Patents Act 1988.

Printed and bound in Great Britain by Clays Ltd, Elcograf S.p.A.
Typeset by Tiger Media

Papers used by Nosy Crow are made from wood grown in
sustainable forests.

ISBN: 978 1 78800 803 7

MIX
Paper from
responsible sources
FSC® C018072

www.nosycrow.com

CHAPTER

ONE

I squeezed through the door of The Wig and Pen, and elbowed a load of bread as somebody jostled me into the shelves. Up ahead, the landlady of the pub-shop climbed on to her bar, tripped over the lemonade tap and landed on Farmer McAndrew's head. The crowd made a collective "whoa!" noise and righted her again.

"What's the town meeting about this time?" I whispered to Kai, my best friend. Nobody had told us yet, but I figured he'd know, seeing as he lived in the flat above our heads.

"Dunno. I've been out on Uncle Doug's boat all morning, setting the lobster traps," he replied with a shrug.

Fabien, my little brother, surveyed the shelf behind me with a sigh. "I've only sold *one* knitted swimming costume! Can you believe it?"

Margot and I looked at each other guiltily, because we were his secret customers, hoping to make him feel better about selling something. We'd given the costume to Farmer McAndrew, who said we were very good big sisters, and then used it to insulate his carrots.

"I'm not sure there's much call for knitted swimming garments in July," I told him.

He shook his head. "I just can't understand it."

"I wish they'd hurry up," said Margot, changing the subject. "I've got a flying lesson at two o'clock."

"And I've got to get back to my goats," said Fabien. "They'll be wanting their cake soon."

Kai stared at him. "You've baked a cake for your pet goats?"

"Yes, because it's been a whole year since we won our island and I became the proud owner of my beautiful herd," said Fabien.

I stared at him, surprised. Had it really been a year since we'd won our island from Mr Billionaire? It only felt like yesterday I'd read about the competition in the newspaper, after we'd found out we were being evicted from our flat in London. I'd only just got used to floating to school on our boat, *Lady Agatha*, rather than being jostled around on the tube.

Everyone chatted loudly as Heidi, the landlady, tried to climb back on to the bar. I looked around and was sure the whole town was here now. It was even busier than last winter's Black Friday, when Heidi (who was also Kai's mum) had given out a free packet of chewing gum with every cucumber bought. She'd run out halfway through the day, resulting in a riot next to the pork scratchings.

Heidi clapped her hands for silence, and Mayor Oddway pole-vaulted on to the bar next to her with a stale French stick. He waved it in the air to get people's attention, and the crowd quietened down, until all that could be heard was the sound of his chains jingling round his neck.

"Are we all here?" he asked.

"Yes!" replied the crowd.

"Excellent. I therefore call this meeting to order," he said. "Now, as you know, planning permission has been applied for by a corporate developer called Gold Rush Properties who want to turn our lovely town of Wishnook into what they are calling 'The Las Vegas of Scotland'! This would mean expanding Windy Nook Airport to accommodate more planes and building a new, faster road between here and the harbour to cope with all the extra traffic. Unfortunately, despite our objections, full planning permission has been granted for this first stage of development. Today I obtained further details about their plans."

I glanced worriedly at Kai, Margot and Fabien,

not knowing what any of this meant. Mum had told me about the development, but I hadn't actually thought it would happen. Why would anyone want to build over the town? It seemed ridiculous.

The mayor unfurled a banner that he'd stashed behind the bar. It looked a bit like one of the collages Fabien liked to do when he got knitter's elbow. I shuffled forward to get a better look, and ended up under Doctor Ted's surprisingly unhygienic-smelling armpit. I wiggled my nose away from the pong and angled myself downwind in the stream of Margot's sweet perfume.

Jumping above the crowd's heads, I saw the banner had CGI drawings of lots of glossy buildings. There was a cloud-grazing hotel, a massive shopping complex and a casino in the shape of an octopus. It was Wishnook Vegas on a roll of partially ripped vinyl.

"Gold Rush Properties are currently looking at sites for a shopping mall, casino and even a theme park," said Mayor Oddway. "Most of you know we have launched a legal appeal against the plans and this will be going to court soon. But we still need to be prepared for the worst. If this goes through, our little town will never be the same again."

Daisy Gifford, the town's one and only journalist, forced her way to the front of the crowd. "Have you thought this might be a *good* thing?" she said.

"Hear, hear!" shouted someone.

"Rubbish!" called someone else.

"These developments bring tourists, and we all know there's been a lack of them lately," continued Daisy. "Our businesses can't survive on thin air. We need to attract holidaymakers and Wishnook's Gold Rush Resort, Spa and Hunting Lodge will do just that. It'll save us all!"

"It'll ruin my business!" said Heidi. "Who's going to want to sup their ale next to a shelf full of toilet cleaner – even if it is the lemon-scented kind – when they can go to a posh wine bar instead?"

There was silence, and then somebody said, "We'll still come here to buy our bread."

"Actually the hotel will include an artisan bakery," said Daisy. "Just think about all the fresh croissants!"

"The extra trade will definitely be good for my orangutans," said Edna, who ran the charity shop.

Margot and I both raised our eyebrows.

"Orangutans?" I said slowly, wondering if Edna had actually lost the plot. Maybe the stress had got to her.

"Yes, I send them the profits from my shop," she said.

Everyone looked away from her and back to Daisy and the mayor, who were stood on opposite sides of the bar looking annoyed with each other.

"Think of the extra tourists that Wishnook Vegas will bring in, though," said Dad. "There'll be more people to buy my seagulls!"

Dad had taken up whittling a few months ago. He said it was something to do with mindfulness, and had built an entire shed in which to work on his new hobby. So far he mostly stuck to whittling seagulls that he kept forcing on people as presents. Kai was the only person who'd escaped being given one, at least for now. His surprise gull weighed heavily in my pocket as I thought about it.

"Nobody will come to my island yoga retreats if there's a fancy hotel for them to stay in instead," said Mum.

"I'm sure people will still come," said Dad soothingly.

Mum scowled at him. "You don't know that. My website will look terrible next to theirs."

"Oi!" said Kai, who'd made it for her. "You've got animated graphics and everything."

Deciding I'd had enough of all the drama, I nodded at Kai to follow me through the hot, sticky crowd outside to the fresh air. Margot and Fabien came tumbling through the door after us, and we raced down to the harbour and dangled our feet in the water to cool down. I watched a seabird bob on the waves and felt like my head was swimming around with it.

Mum had tried not to worry us about the development, but without her yoga retreats we'd all go hungry again unless we learned how to fish.

"We must find a way to stop this happening," I said.

"We could start a petition?" suggested Kai.

"No, we need to do something bigger than that," I said.

"Can't you ask Mr Billionaire? I mean, he wouldn't want to see this happen to Wishnook, would he?" said Kai.

"He's travelling," I replied.

It had been six months since Mr Billionaire had last visited us. He'd gone on a year-long expedition to Antarctica with a pack of huskies and a boatful of scientists. I wasn't quite sure what he was doing there. The last time we'd seen him, he'd just mentioned something about liking snow and igloos. I hoped he'd taken a good coat with him.

"Maybe Daisy's right, and this resort won't be such a bad thing," said Margot. "I could get a job there and put money towards my flying lessons. Plus, they're going to invest in the airport!"

"You're fourteen," I reminded her.

"But I'll be sixteen by the time it's finished," she said.

"What about Mum's yoga retreats? What if she goes out of business?" I asked.

"We'll grow cabbages," said Margot.

I wasn't convinced. If Mum went out of business, that would mean no more food, no oil for the generator that made our light bulbs work, no peat for the fire and no fuel for our boat, *Lady Agatha*. It would mean no more living on our island, unless Dad could sell a million whittled seagulls or Fabien could start a trend for knitted underwear. Both seemed quite unlikely.

Worse, it would mean I'd have to close my donkey sanctuary.

I'd opened my donkey sanctuary at the end of last summer and now had three rescue donkeys. The last one, Sunshine, had been given up when her owner had moved country. She was the littlest donkey but the boldest too – unless she had to go near a beach, which was a bit of a problem as her new home was an island.

I couldn't close my sanctuary! I'd promised Monty, Moon and Sunshine that they'd finally found their forever homes. I couldn't go back on my word. They needed me.

I turned to Fabien. "You're on our side, aren't you?"

"Well … it *would* be nice to expand my knitting business," he replied. "Besides, paintballing looks really fun."

Now I was confused. "What do you mean?"

"Something on Mayor Oddway's poster said *shooting range*," he said.

Kai shook his head. "That's not paintballing. That means *goose* shooting."

The colour drained from Fabien's usually bright face. "You mean … shooting *real* geese? With *real* guns? Not firing paint at people's bottoms?"

"Yes," I said.

He gripped the harbour wall. "That's *horrible.*"

"Actually," began Kai, "the geese around here *are* kind of pests. They're constantly trying to eat all the farm crops, and they swallowed one of Uncle Doug's best socks once when he was drying them outside his boat shack."

The colour returned to Fabien's face, but this time he turned so red that he resembled a beetroot. "You wouldn't shoot me if *I* ate your Uncle Doug's socks, would you?"

Kai considered this. "It depends why you'd eaten it. I mean, if you were a sock-eating zombie, then, yeah, probably. But if you got confused and thought it was a smoked kipper, then obviously not. They do smell kind of similar."

"Can we stop talking about socks and get back to the point?" I asked.

"What was the point again?" said Kai, looking a bit lost.

"That we have to save the town!" I replied. "Who's with me?"

I held out my hand, and Kai and Fabien piled theirs on top. "We are!" they both chirped.

Margot sat on her hands and looked pointedly up at the clouds. I took out the whittled seagull from my pocket and pecked her on the hand with it. She made an *ouch* sound, then shuffled away. I huffed. She'd change her mind when she'd thought about it more.

We needed Margot on our side. After all, she could fly real aeroplanes and explain what a subordinate conjunction was, *and* name all the planets without doing the rhyme in her head first. All I could do was worm a donkey.

Footsteps whacked on the pavement behind us, and I turned to find Mum panting and doubled over.

"What's wrong, Mrs Butterworth?" asked Kai.

"Are the developers here already?" I said. "Should we lie down in front of the diggers?"

"That sounds dangerous…" replied Fabien, his face scrunched with worry.

Mum shook her head. "It's the yoga guests," she wheezed. "I've just remembered I was supposed to pick them up at lunchtime, but with all the commotion about today's meeting I completely forgot!"

"So where are they now?" asked Margot.

Mum shrugged desperately.

Oh no! We'd lost the yoga guests!

CHAPTER

TWO

"What do they look like?" asked Kai.

"They'll be dressed in Lycra; they always are," I told him.

"Yes, and they'll have babies," said Mum, chasing after us.

"What babies?" asked Margot.

"This is the new baby-yoga week I'm trialling," she said.

"Oh, the one where parents waft babies above their heads and then balance them on their feet?" I said.

Mum nodded. "Yes."

"Oh, I forgot you're doing that," said Margot.

"I hope the babies don't scare my goats," said Fabien. "They're sensitive to change."

I threw myself on to my bike, which I kept in Kai's yard, and cycled up the high street with him. The others spread out across the harbour to cover more ground. Closed signs loomed across the doors of all the little shops and businesses I pedalled past. There was a big poster in the Wishnook butcher's advertising their discounted sausages: *Buy our bangers! Six for sixty (pence)!* The window of the charity shop next door was filled with dust, and didn't look like it had seen a soul for months. There was a gift shop with a closing-down sign in the window, and a bakery that only opened in the mornings now. It was like cycling through a ghost town.

"Where would you go if you were a baby?" I asked.

"Somewhere with sugar," replied Kai, and then we both looked at each other.

Mr Percy's pop-up ice-cream stall!

Mr Percy's ice-cream stall was at the top of the hill and was made from a wallpapering table with a cutlery drawer glued underneath. As I cycled towards it, I could see a line of people snaking away from it, each with a small, squirming bundle in their arms.

"Look, over there!" I yelled at Kai.

Mr Percy beamed and waved at us. "I've just sold seven and a half ice creams! This is the most business I've done all summer!" he shouted.

I waved back and skidded to a halt in front of the ice-cream eaters. They were all dressed in sportswear, and the wiggling bundles were definitely babies. One of the babies had a wafer cone on its head, and there was a puddle of melted chocolate at its mother's feet. I reached into my pocket and passed her a tissue.

After I'd introduced myself, Kai and I herded the yoga guests down the street and on to Lady Agatha. It was a tight squeeze with everyone on the boat, and I ended up sitting on top of a box of teething powder. Dad started the engine, and I waved goodbye to Kai. The boat crashed heavily across the water, and Lady Agatha's engine strained under the weight. I tried to shuffle away from the yoga babies, who were giggling, crying or throwing up in sync. One made a horrific farting noise, and then fell asleep peacefully in her father's arms, tummy gurgling menacingly. Margot held her nose and scowled.

"Luna will make you some refreshments while my husband and I bring in the luggage," said Mum, when we docked back at the island.

"Will she?" I asked.

"Yes, she will," muttered Mum.

I glanced longingly across the beach at my donkeys, then led the yoga people in the direction of our house.

"This is beautiful," said one of the ladies, and her baby scowled at a goat as we passed. Margot and Fabien followed the parents like collies herding sheep.

"Reminds me of some of the locations I've filmed in," said one of the men.

"Filmed?" I asked him. "Are you a movie star?"

"Not quite," he chuckled. "I'm a runner for *Wild Countryside*."

"The TV show?"

"That's right," he replied.

I'd heard of *Wild Countryside* before. It was one of those boring teatime programmes that old people liked, about sheep, and grass, and blackcurrant jam. I used to turn it over when we had a TV, but Dad loved it and sometimes still watched it if we went to The Wig and Pen for tea.

"What's a TV runner?" asked Fabien. "Do you run around with TVs, like a challenge?"

The man, who said he was called Greg, laughed again, and his baby hiccupped. "Close. I run around doing errands – fetching coffee and helping people with their lines. Hopefully I'll be in front of the cameras one day, but for now it's not a bad job."

"Must be stressful, though," mused somebody else.

"A little. That's why I've come here for a break. Yoga is very relaxing, and little Vera likes it."

"You named your baby *Little Vera*?" said Fabien in a tone that barely hid how appalled he was.

"You're a fine one to talk about names," hissed Margot, as we passed Violet Pansy Hyacinth the Third, one of his goats.

"*I'm* named after a footballer," said Fabien proudly, despite the fact he couldn't kick a ball to save his life. "And Luna's named after the crazy girl from *Harry Potter*."

"What about you?" Greg asked Margot.

"Mum named me after the doctor who delivered me," said Margot. "She thought I might get a good job if I had a posh name."

We reached our house in the middle of the island and I led the yoga guests into the mansion's living room, then shut myself in the peacefulness of the kitchen with Margot and Fabien.

"I'm going to show them my catalogue of swimming costumes," said Fabien.

"Let them get settled in first," said Margot.

I stared out of the kitchen window and thought about how amazing working for a TV show would be. Maybe I could get a job on a programme about donkeys or islands. The idea flittered out of my head as quickly as it had arrived. Most adults thought eleven was too young to work, and I couldn't be away from my donkeys for longer than a day.

Then it came to me: a new idea that made my tummy fizz with excitement.

"We should make a movie about our animals!" I said. "Wouldn't you want to see the world's most talented goats?"

Margot shook her head. "No."

But Fabien was jumping up and down in excitement. "We're going to be famous!"

"I know!" I yelled. "And it wouldn't just have to be about our animals. It could be about our island, and The Wig and Pen, and Mr Percy's ice-cream stall. It could be about the whole town!"

"But why?" asked Margot.

"We can show it to the judge when the appeal goes to court. He'll have to stop them developing Wishnook when he sees how amazing our home is already!"

"But you don't know the first thing about making a movie," replied Margot.

"We'll ask Greg," said Fabien.

"That's ... actually genius," I said, surprised.

Fabien beamed with pride.

"What about a camera?" asked Margot.

"We'll borrow one from somebody," I said.

Margot shook her head again. "I have to go," she said. "Airbus have released a new plane and I need to study the flight manual." And with that she left.

I poured myself some orange juice in my donkey mug and wondered when it was exactly that Margot had stopped being fun.

CHAPTER

THREE

I set my alarm for early the next morning. There were only twelve days until the appeal went to court. I didn't have a second to lose if I was going to save the town.

The first thing I needed to do was find a camera. After all, it would be a bit hard to make a movie without one. I was sure we had one somewhere in the house, but four broom cupboards and eighteen drawers later there was no sign of the old thing. Maybe we'd given it away before we'd moved. Mum had sold loads of our stuff when Dad had been sad, to try to pay the rent on our old flat. Now I thought about it I was sure the camera was one of them.

"What are you doing?" asked Mum, as I brushed a decade's worth of dust off my knees.

I told her all about our movie plan, while Dad hovered in the background, varnishing the hallway's wooden panelling.

"What a brilliant idea!" cried Mum.

Dad dropped his brush. "I'm not sure about this…"

"That's because you're on the developers' side," replied Mum curtly.

"You'll upset half the town," he told me.

Before I could reply, Mum and Dad launched into a debate about Wishnook Vegas, which resulted in both of them being covered in copious amounts of orange varnish. I tutted at them and continued my search for the camera.

It was almost mid-morning before I finally gave up looking. I raided my piggy bank and counted up the money. There was just about enough to buy an old camera from the charity shop, if Edna had one in stock. It probably wouldn't be very good, but I was sure Kai could edit the footage on his computer and make it look all swanky.

I poured the money into my coin purse, and went to Dad's shed to ask for a lift. He was in there, wiping the last remaining varnish off his forehead with a bottle of surgical spirit. A flock of wooden seagulls swung above his head.

"Can you take me to the mainland so I can see Kai?" I asked.

"All right. I need to get some lamb for tonight's stew anyway," he said.

Fabien, who was walking past the shed, stopped in his tracks and shot daggers at us. "We DO NOT eat lamb on this island."

"Sorry, sorry, I meant lentils," said Dad hurriedly.

I filled Fabien in on my plan to find a camera, and the pair of us climbed into *Lady Agatha*, ready to set sail. Luckily Margot was busy revising for her pilot's licence test, even though she couldn't take it yet. I didn't want her to find out about the camera and start interfering. The less she knew about our movie the better, seeing as she didn't want to help with it.

I held on to *Lady Agatha* as Dad started the engine and we clonked out to sea. A leak sprang at the stern, where a cork had popped loose. We grabbed a plastic tea set out of the picnic basket, which Mum kept on board for such occasions, and began scooping the water out.

Dad moored up next to Doug's boat shack and set about repairing the leak with him, while Fabien and I raced towards The Wig and Pen. I couldn't wait to tell Kai all about our movie, but there was no sign of him inside the deserted pub-shop, so I went off to find him out the back.

Sure enough, Kai was sat in the little courtyard. He was surrounded by his rescue rabbits, the inspiration for my own donkey sanctuary. I picked my way through the sea of twitching noses, and Fabien cuddled a lop-ear called Julio. A rabbit hopped over to me and I gave him a dandelion while filling Kai in on our idea. The toothless rabbit slurped its snack like an old man eating spaghetti.

"So, what do you think?" I asked Kai, after explaining everything.

"I think the movie's a great idea!" he said. "We could film my play for it too."

Of course, Kai's play! I'd forgotten all about it in the excitement.

Kai's dad used to run the Wishnook Community Theatre in his spare time, but it had fallen into disrepair after he'd died. Kai had spent the last six months getting it ready to reopen and had written a play for the town to perform at the end of summer. He was intending to hold auditions later that week for the parts of Venus the planet and Spartacus the Roman alien.

"I might have to shorten the performance time a bit, though…" he mused.

"Why, how long is it?" I asked, as a rabbit nibbled my shoe.

"About three hours and ten minutes at the last

script read-through," said Kai. "Mum reckons it should be more like forty-five minutes, so I might have to cut the underwater scenes."

"Underwa— Never mind," I said. "Can you help me look for a camera? We need to get started with everything right away."

"Don't need to. I've got one upstairs we can use. Mum bought it for me when I needed to film an advert for the rabbit rescue."

Excitement bubbled up in me when Kai brought the camera downstairs. It looked really fancy, with a large lens that zoomed out when he turned it on. Kai pointed the camera at me and it beeped as he pressed the button on the top. I stood over his shoulder and saw that it was recording.

"It shoots in 4K," he said.

"Margot's going to hate it," muttered Fabien.

Kai turned off the camera and handed it to me. It was perfect! Now we had a story and something to film it on.

I led Kai back to *Lady Agatha* so we could get started with filming on the island. Doug was stooped over on the deck, repairing the leak by bashing at something with a shoe. I glanced around for Dad and saw him wandering back across the harbour, carrying a paper parcel from the butcher's. I peered at it as he climbed on board. It looked suspiciously shaped like a lamb leg, but I didn't say anything. Maybe Fabien would just think it was a bag of potatoes.

We set off back to the island on the newly patched-up boat. I sat by the hole with my teacup, ready to start bailing, but *Lady Agatha* managed to make it back to the island without any more leaks. Dad patted the steering wheel proudly as we climbed out, and I went to test the camera properly.

I spotted Sunshine at the edge of the woods looking at the sand anxiously, and zoomed the lens in on her. She was a particularly beautiful donkey, and her eyes sparkled on the camera screen. I kept the lens focused on her as I ran over and climbed on to her back.

"What are you doing?" asked Kai.

"I'm going to record a tour of the island on donkey-back!" I said.

I panned the camera around. Further down the beach, Mum and her yoga guests were wobbling on one leg. I zoomed in on them and then back out to the ocean, where little fishing boats bobbed serenely on the calm water.

"Record this crab shell!" yelled Fabien, tearing over to me with a tiny crab in his hands.

Sand flicked up from his feet, and he thrust the crab shell up towards me. Sunshine flattened her ears and took a step back. I felt her stumble and glanced down, just in time to see a goat skip out from under her legs. It lowered its horns and head-butted Sunshine in the bottom, annoyed at having been stood on.

Sunshine stomped her hooves and lurched forward on to the beach. I grabbed on to her stubby mane with one hand while trying to keep the camera steady in the other.

"It's OK!" I whispered to her, but I saw Sunshine look at the sand beneath her hooves and felt the horror ripple through her. Before I could do anything, she broke into a freaked-out gallop, careering down the beach faster than a missile. The camera jerked, but I managed to keep filming, wrapping my legs round Sunshine so tightly they went tingly.

Kai shouted something behind me. I couldn't hear what it was, but his voice sounded panicked.

I squeezed my eyes shut and hoped we weren't about to die.

"Watch out!" I heard him say, just managing to make out the words.

I opened one eye and saw we were heading straight towards Mum and the yoga people, who were crumpled together further up the beach.

"Get out of the way!" I yelled at her.

Mum untangled herself from the pretzel pose she'd been in and screamed. The yoga people, who were waving their babies above their heads like a scene from The Lion King, looked around in panic. Vera burst into tears, coughed and regurgitated broccoli on to Greg's head. It dripped into his eyes, over the end of his nose, and landed with a splatter on the sand.

The yoga people rolled out of Sunshine's way, and she screeched to a halt in front of Mum.

"Luna, get your donkey out of here!" she yelled. "And somebody get Greg a baby wipe for goodness' sake!"

Greg wiped his eye with a clump of seaweed. "I'm OK. I don't think she's blinded me."

Margot stepped out from the trees behind me, covered in engine oil from some kind of project, eyebrows raised. "I see your movie's going well. Hollywood here you come," she said.

I only just resisted the urge to throw regurgitated broccoli at her head.

CHAPTER

FOUR

Mum grounded me for the rest of the afternoon, even though it wasn't my fault that Sunshine had nearly killed her. I couldn't just spend the afternoon doing nothing, though, so I locked myself away in my room and started making a list of things to film. We'd need to record the fish market and its massive prawn things, and the fishing people, and the nearby farms and shops, and The Wig and Pen's quiz. And we needed to interview people too – important people like the mayor, because the judge might listen to him.

By dinner time I had an entire storyboard of things to shoot, but it was too late to get started. I kept the ideas under my pillow as I slept that night, hoping they might bake away in my head.

"Can you drop me off at the mainland?" I said, over breakfast.

"Not today," replied Dad, bursting my bubble. "It's the first day of the Matt Butterworth Summer School of Excellence."

Margot, Fabien and I all dropped our toast, and I nearly fell off my kitchen stool.

"The Matt Butterworth..." I began to repeat, but the words were too hideous to say aloud.

Fabien shook with what I guessed was either rage or fear. "*School? In the summer*?!" he exclaimed.

Dad grinned. "It's going to be fun! I've got it all planned out!"

I crossed my arms. "But it's the summer holidays. You can't make us learn stuff in the *summer*!"

"Exactly," said Margot, and I felt relieved that we were agreeing on something. "I wanted to write a CV and send it to the Gold Rush people today."

"You can't do that. They're the enemy!" I yelled.

"It's just a job application," said Margot, and went off to complain about Dad's school to Mum.

"You're only doing this school thing because you don't want us to make our movie," I told Dad. "It's sabotage!"

"That's not true. I'm doing this because it's educational," he replied.

I snorted. This was an absolute disaster! There were only eleven days until the court case. We didn't have time to mess around with silly things like school. I couldn't afford to waste an entire day.

Five seconds later, the kitchen door swung

open, and Kai marched in wearing a pair of old shorts and muddy wellies.

"What are you doing here?" I asked him.

"Apparently I'm here for summer school," he said, glaring at Dad.

Dad waved and scraped a blackened pancake on to a plate for him. "I'm so glad you could make it. Where are the others?"

"Others? What others?!" I shrieked.

Right on cue, a literal stampede hurtled into the kitchen. I groaned. It was the entire child population of Wishnook. Harper glared at me and mouthed, "You're dead." Caleb ignored us all and headed straight to the pancakes, while Liam slumped to the floor and went back to sleep.

Fabien and I fought our way through the crowd, and went to join Margot in harassing Mum. We found her down at the beach, lying on the warming sand. Mum was trying to teach the yoga guests to meditate while the babies chewed shells and pebbles and bits of seaweed. Margot was lying next to Mum, prodding her in the arm and whispering, "Save us, save us, save us," over and over on a loop.

I picked my way across a stream of drool, which

I hoped belonged to the babies and not their parents, and crouched next to Mum too.

"Save us, save us, save us from school," I whispered into her other ear.

Fabien poked her ribcage, and a baby crawled over and pinched Mum on the nose.

"Deep, cleansing breaths!" Mum told the yoga guests through gritted teeth.

"This is useless," sighed Margot. "Have you got any idea how we're going to get out of this?"

"Have you changed your mind about working for Gold Rush Properties?" I asked.

"No, there's nobody else I can work for around here," she replied.

"Then we can't help you, can we, Fabien?" I said.

Fabien looked uneasy at having to pick sides.

Just then, I heard Dad call to us from the top of the hill that led down to the beach. I squinted through the sunlight, and saw his hostages dragging their feet behind him. Kai was right at the back, looking around like a wild thing, clearly trying to set upon an escape plan.

Now it was Mum's turn to jab us in the ribs. "Go on, off you pop," she told us.

I staggered to my feet and met Dad and his class halfway down the hill. To my horror I noticed everyone was carrying clipboards with those little pencils attached. Dad was actually, really, properly planning on getting us to do work.

"What exactly are we doing?" I asked, as he handed me, Margot and Fabien a clipboard each.

"Beachcombing," he replied. "We're going to note down what we find and look it up in the encyclopaedia."

"Oh, that sounds fun!" shouted Fabien, and then added, "What's an encyclopaedia?"

"I think it's like Wikipedia but slower," I said.

Fabien didn't look impressed.

"Let's get started," announced Dad. "You can comb the beach in pairs if you want."

Margot and I both looked at each other awkwardly. The idea of pairing up together made the hairs on my arms bristle. I glanced around, and saw Kai wave at me from behind the pack. I hurried away from Margot like she was made of brambles.

"What's up with you two?" he asked, as we set off across the beach.

"She still wants to work at Wishnook Vegas,"

I said. "I can't believe she'd risk our island for a job finding golf balls."

I glanced back at Margot and Fabien, who were combing the sand together.

"I've found a toothbrush!" shouted Fabien. "I think it's been used!"

"Eww!" shouted somebody else.

"Cool!" said another.

I stooped down and grabbed a handful of sand, although I wasn't really looking for anything. The tiny grains trickled through my fingers, and I wondered how old they were, and where they'd come from. Would there still be any sand left after Gold Rush Properties had finished turning Wishnook into a concrete jungle?

There was a shout from somebody further down the beach. "I've found a baby!" Liam yelled. "Ouch, it bit me!"

"Here you go, I've found a plaster!" Harper said.

"Just put it back where you found it," called Dad.

"The baby or the plaster?" asked Harper.

"Both!" he yelled.

By the time we'd finished combing the beach

we'd found several babies, plasters, toothbrushes, half a windscreen wiper, two metres of rope, a Lego dinosaur, some poo (donkey and goat) and a bottle (without a message). There was also a shell, which Dad thought belonged to a hermit crab, but which actually turned out to be a rather disgusting sea snail.

Fabien bounded up to me. "I found a fish skeleton! Margot trod on its head, but it's still intact."

"Oh ... that's ... lovely," I said.

"Delightful," added Margot, but I still couldn't look at her.

I'd hoped school was over for the day, but then Dad shepherded us in the direction of the rock pools for more beachcombing. I slipped away while he was distracted, and took a shortcut across the woodland to check on my donkeys. Monty was grazing on one of the many saplings that Margot had recently planted. She said she'd done it to stop Fabien lecturing her about carbon emissions, although I'd caught her talking to them when she thought nobody was looking, encouraging them to grow. She'd even knocked up a couple of birdhouses in Dad's shed for when the trees were big enough to support them, so I knew my nice sister was still in there somewhere.

The others had already reached the rock pools by the time I caught up, but instead of scrabbling around searching for treasure, they were gathered together, murmuring loudly and pointing at something.

"What's happening?" I asked, squeezing through.

I stopped in my tracks. Huge sheets of thick, hard-looking plastic were lying across the pools. There must have been at least a hundred of the things, probably more. I didn't understand what they were, or where they'd come from.

"It looks like some sort of wall cladding," said Dad.

"Must have fallen off a cargo ship," said Kai, and he grabbed the camera that was hanging round my neck and filmed it.

"What are we going to do? There are too many to move. What if there are crabs or fish trapped under them?" I asked.

Dad inspected the cladding. "I'll have to go to the mainland and ask if anyone knows where it's come from. Go back to the house, kids."

There was a loud chorus of protest, but Dad herded everyone away from the pools, waving his clipboard menacingly.

"Do you think it's connected to Gold Rush Properties?"

"Let's find out," said Kai, and we tiptoed quietly away.

CHAPTER

FIVE

The discovery of the cladding meant the end of that day's summer school. Dad radioed the mainland and Doug came to collect the children in his boat taxi, much to everybody's joy. Mum cut her yoga class short, her face beetroot red when she saw the plastic for herself.

"Can we come too?" I asked Dad, who was readying *Lady Agatha* for the mainland. He wanted to try to find out where the cladding had come from, although nobody quite knew how he was going to do it. There wasn't much in the way of CCTV in the ocean.

"OK, you can look out for any more floating debris," he replied.

Kai, Fabien, Mum and I climbed into the boat, along with Margot, who was missing WIFI. The yoga guests looked relieved as they waved us goodbye, exhausted from their relaxing yoga session.

The journey to the mainland felt like it took twice as long as normal. All I wanted to do was find out who was responsible for littering our rock pools.

As soon as we docked, Kai and I grabbed our bikes from The Wig and Pen. We didn't even wait for Mum and Dad to find Mayor Oddway. I couldn't wait another second.

"What are you doing?" asked Margot, as Fabien climbed on to the back of my muddy BMX.

"We're going up to the resort, to see if the cladding came from there," I said.

"I'll come too," said Margot.

I wasn't sure Margot coming was a good idea. She might grab a shovel and start building the hotel herself. On the other hand, though, if the cladding had come from Gold Rush Properties, maybe it would be enough to change her mind about getting a job there. I decided it was worth the gamble and fished a half-broken bike out from behind a rabbit hutch for her.

"A bike? This isn't the nineteen seventies," said Margot.

"You could always walk," suggested Kai.

Margot seemed to consider this, but then reluctantly hopped on to the bike. She gripped the handlebars and wobbled as she tried to sit down. I couldn't remember when Margot had last ridden a bike. We never had much chance in London, and she'd not been near one since we'd moved. She looked even rustier at it than

I'd been, when I'd borrowed that very same bike last year.

It took Margot a couple of minutes to get her balance, but once she'd assessed the mechanics of the bike she seemed suddenly much more stable.

"Right, I think I'm ready," she said. "Although this would be so much better if it had an engine, or at least a battery."

We pointed our bikes in the direction of the McAndrews' farm and pedalled across the harbour. I stared at the fields and cows, thinking about how beautiful it all was, until we reached the little dirt track that led to the farm. For every pothole Kai and I swerved, Margot let out a yelp as she hurtled into it and bounced back out. I tried not to laugh as she gasped rude words and, between pants, began a long speech about exactly why Heidi's bike was so aerodynamically inefficient.

Farmer McAndrew had sold off some land at the back of his farm years ago and it had been unused ever since. It was ringed by a tall hedge, which now appeared to have something covering it. As we got closer, I realised it was a tightly woven net slung over the twigs. It was made of green string that blended into the leaves and tangled menacingly round the branches. It stretched for as far as we could see.

Kai's face turned a deep, dark red. "They've netted the hedgerows!"

"Why?" asked Fabien, hopping off my bike. "That's just silly. Where will the birds go?"

Margot bit her lip. "This must be a mistake."

Kai got his camera out and Fabien started to pull at the netting. A little red bird suddenly sprang out and wobbled into the sky, its wings crumpled. The sight of it made sad, angry tears spring to my eyes. How many other birds were trapped behind the horrible net?

I pressed my feet to the pedals and set off again, leaving Fabien and Kai to wrestle with the net. Behind me, I could hear Margot pedalling too, her brakes screeching every few seconds.

The netted hedgerow stretched on for ages, until we finally reached a gate that led into the fields beyond. I hopped off my bike and pushed it open. Dozens of shipping containers were lined up on the other side, and beyond them was a Portakabin plonked in the middle of the yellow-green grass. On the horizon a convoy of diggers and dumper trucks were parked up, lying in wait. My heart beat noisily. It looked like work on the resort had already begun.

"Oi, clear off!" shouted a voice. "This is private land."

A man appeared from behind one of the shipping containers, and I recognised him as a regular from The Wig and Pen. His name was Jamie and he was a builder. I knew that because he always kept his hard hat on when he drank in the pub-shop because he didn't trust the roof. I'd never really spoken to him much more than that, but I knew he'd fixed the door of Doug's boat shack for free when it had broken during a storm last winter.

"Oh, it's you," he said, when he got closer. "What are you doing up here? It's not safe with all the deliveries."

"Are you working here?" I asked him.

Jamie nodded. "Yes, I'm the foreman."

I wasn't really sure what a foreman was, but it sounded rather important. Was Jamie responsible for netting the hedges? I couldn't believe anyone who lived in the countryside, who saw all the birds, mice, badgers and deer every day, would want to harm it like that.

"Have you already started work on the resort?" asked Margot, taking in all the trucks.

"We're just getting everything ready," he replied.

The bad feeling in my tummy grew heavier. Gold Rush Properties really did mean business. If our movie wasn't a success, and the appeal failed, Jamie and his workers would start building the very next day. What if we weren't good enough to stop them? What if the planning people thought our movie was rubbish and we were all talentless and that Wishnook was worthless? Could we really stop all of this?

Margot pointed to the netting on the hedge. "What's all that about?"

"It's standard procedure," said Jamie. "We can only get permission to cut the hedgerow down if there are no birds' nests in there, and nets keep the birds out."

My face grew hot. "But there are animals trapped in it!"

"I'm only following orders." He shrugged.

Just as I thought I might explode, a car honked

behind us and I spun round. I wondered if it was the big boss getting ready to drag us off his land. Instead, Daisy Gifford and Mayor Oddway got out of the car. Dad and Mum scrambled from the back seats after them.

Daisy instantly began snapping photos of the netting, while Mayor Oddway marched up to Jamie and took him off for a private talk. Mum shook her head at the netting, then grabbed a fistful and started pulling at it too. I joined in and looked over at Margot, who was frozen to the spot.

"Aren't you going to help?" I said to her and Dad.

I could see Margot weighing her pilot-licence dream up against the trapped birds. If she helped, the Gold Rush people might not give her a job. But if she didn't, it was like agreeing with what they'd done.

"It does make sense to net the hedges, if they're going to remove them," said Dad. "Might be safer for the animals."

"Safer?" I said. "How would you like it if I put a net across your bedroom door, so you couldn't leave?"

Mum glanced at me worriedly. "Please don't."

I turned to Margot. "You can't think this is OK," I said.

Margot bit her lip, and then made to turn away from me.

I dropped the net in shock. "Are you leaving?" I yelled at her.

She ignored me, and without looking back went over to Jamie and Mayor Oddway. I tore at the netting even faster, the anger bubbling out through my hands. The strings cut into my fingers, as I yanked harder. Margot was probably asking for a job right now. I couldn't believe it!

I heard the click of Kai's bicycle wheels and saw him and Fabien bump through the hedge. Fabien looked like he might pass out from exhaustion.

"We need something to cut the netting with," said Kai, as he got out his camera and pressed record again.

"Maybe we can sneak something from one of those shipping containers," I said, but then got distracted by Margot and the foreman again.

I couldn't hear what they were saying but I watched as Jamie took out his phone and pressed it to his ear, while Margot and Mayor Oddway continued talking to each other. I hoped she wasn't trying to convince him this was all OK.

After what felt like years, the foreman put his phone back in his pocket and walked over to us. I abandoned my plan to sneak into a shipping container, and waited for him to open his mouth.

"I've spoken to my superior, and he's agreed to take down the nets, provided you don't print any of this in the *Gazette*," he said to Daisy, as she flashed her camera in his face.

Daisy lowered the lens. "I can't do that; this will shift loads of papers! But I can publish a nice photo of the hedges when they're all back to normal, and a little interview with you."

"An interview with me..." said Jamie thoughtfully, and I was sure I saw his chest puff out a bit. "All right, Daisy, you've got a deal."

Then I remembered why we were here in the first place. "There's loads of plastic cladding washing up on our island. It must be something to do with the resort. What are you going to do about it?" I said.

"*If* it's ours, somebody will be along to collect it and bring it back here," replied Jamie, waving his hand dismissively.

Margot came over. "See, I told you they weren't monsters."

"What were you saying to Jamie?"

"Just that the nets won't help people come round to the idea of the resort," said Margot. "It doesn't make sense to upset people."

"And they agreed to take them down, just like that?" I asked.

"They don't want any trouble before the appeal," said Margot.

I wasn't sure I could trust Jamie to remove the nets but Margot genuinely seemed to believe him. I wondered whether this meant we were on the same side now. Maybe seeing what building the resort actually meant had made her change her mind about it.

I loosened my grip on the net. Even if they did take it down, the fields were already starting to look like a construction yard. All the shipping containers, pipes and trucks must have cost thousands. Gold Rush Properties were obviously richer even than Mr Billionaire. I wondered how Kai, Fabien and I were supposed to fight them, armed only with a camera. Suddenly the whole idea seemed impossible. Adults in charge never listen to kids.

Kai swept his camera around the hedges. "I've recorded it all for our movie. This will show the planning judge how horrible the developers are."

"What movie?" asked Daisy, ears burning.

"Nothing!" I yelled.

The last thing we needed was Daisy finding out about it. She'd probably find a way to stop us, or sabotage things.

"We're making a movie about why Wishnook is so brilliant, and we're going to show it to the planning people so they stop Wishnook Vegas," blurted out Fabien.

I groaned. He was about as useless at keeping secrets as a colander is at keeping in water.

Daisy's eyes grew wide. "Are you now...? How very interesting..." She was practically purring.

"This is bad," muttered Kai.

I knew he was right.

CHAPTER

SIX

"Your baby's in the recycling again," I said to one of the yoga guests the next morning.

The lady scooped up her baby and plucked a cereal box off his head. "Oops."

"What are we doing today?" asked Fabien.

"I thought we could go to the fish market," replied Mum. "Fabien, Dad can take you to The Wig and Pen for scrambled tofu afterwards."

"Yummy!" said Fabien.

"Revolting," said Margot. At least Margot and I still agreed about something.

We piled into *Lady Agatha*, yoga guests and all. I hoped we wouldn't see Daisy. The idea of her knowing about our movie made my tummy feel like it was full of big pebbles. I really hoped she wouldn't try to interfere or stop us. We had everything left to film and no time for sabotage.

Mum started the boat's engine, but stopped when one of the guests realised they'd forgotten their baby and had to go back to the house for her. With the neglected child rounded up, we finally set out to sea.

We were about halfway towards the mainland when we passed our first fishing boat. I waved at its captain. He leaned overboard and tossed us a mackerel from his catch. It landed on my foot and slid down the deck into Margot's rucksack.

"Not again," she grumbled, pulling it out by its tail and throwing it into Mum's handbag instead.

Mum smiled at the captain. "Thanks, Shawn! That'll be lovely on a bit of buttery toast!"

We collected another mackerel from the next boat we passed. The locals liked to feed us in exchange for weekly yoga lessons with Mum. I guessed maybe we wouldn't quite go hungry if Mum's yoga business went bankrupt, but I didn't much fancy just eating fish for the rest of my life.

By the time we reached the mainland Mum's handbag was bulging with glossy fish. They were starting to whiff a bit, even through the cloud of Margot's perfume.

I hopped off the boat. The fish market was already crowded. In a town where nothing much ever happened it was the social highlight of the week. Most people went more to have a natter over a cup of whelks than to actually buy anything. That day, though, the market seemed to be even busier than normal. My heart sank when I saw Daisy's head bob above the crowd.

"We've got to hide from her," I said to Fabien.

I weaved between the smelly stalls and spotted Kai plonking fish into a box for The Wig and Pen. He waved a sea trout at me, and I hurried over to him.

"Has Daisy mentioned anything to you about the movie? Is she going to try to stop us making it?" I asked. "What about the nets? Are they still up?"

"Whoa, slow down," he replied. "Daisy hasn't said anything about the movie, although the word on the street is that she's planning to make some sort of announcement this morning. Mum's bringing the karaoke machine over for her so she can use the mic."

That didn't sound good. What did Daisy want to say? I was sure it was about our movie. The heavy feeling in my tummy grew even heavier.

"But the nets have gone," said Kai, which made me feel happier.

"Oh, well, that's something, I guess," I said.

If we could get the nets taken down, maybe we really *could* stop the development? An unexpected spark of hope fizzed through me. Perhaps we could do this after all!

I took out my camera to film the market, hoping to stay out of Daisy's sight. If the development *did* go ahead, a big road was going to be built right through the market and all the stalls would have to move or close down. We needed to show the judge how important the market was to everyone and that it shouldn't be tarmacked over.

"Wonderful! You've brought the camera!" said Daisy from seemingly nowhere. "Make sure you capture my best side."

Fabien, who was buying seaweed from the stall next to us, stopped and scrutinised Daisy's face. "I'd say it's your left one. Your make-up's a bit weird on the other side."

Daisy narrowed her eyes at him. "It's supposed to be like that."

"Oh..." said Fabien. "Then why say you've got a best side?" And then he returned to picking strands of green plant life.

Heidi came over with a karaoke machine trailing behind her and handed the microphone to Daisy. Daisy grinned, jaws wide like a snake with a mouse, and clambered on to one of the fish stalls.

"Oi, watch the salmon!" the stallholder yelled,

and whipped a dead-eyed fish out from under her foot.

"Attention, everyone!" Daisy yelled into the karaoke machine's microphone. "Now, I know some of you have heard the rumours about the Wishnook movie, and I want to confirm they're true. The Butterworth children and Kai have decided to make a movie about our town to influence the judge and stop Gold Rush Properties building their resort."

I felt everyone's eyes on me, and my skin went hot.

"Good for them!" somebody from the crowd shouted.

Another person laughed unkindly. "A movie? They're not exactly Stephen Spielberg."

Fabien crossed his arms. "We're better than him!" he yelled, offended. Then he turned to me and whispered, "Who's Stephen Spellberg?"

Daisy cleared her throat to grab the attention back. "Although I'm sure supporters of the development don't need to worry about this amateur movie, I have decided to make my own to show to the judge at the same time. It will prove why this new resort is a *good* thing for the town. I have a sign-up sheet here for anyone that wants to be in it."

I dropped the camera in shock but Kai retrieved it from the floor and continued filming. Daisy was making her own movie, and it was going to go head-to-head with ours at the court case! I bet she'd have a really good camera too, being a journalist, and a fancy laptop with fancy moviemaking software. She probably knew exactly how to record a movie. I bet she even had some sort of qualification in it. How were Fabien, Kai and I meant to compete with that?

Kai's camera was good, but the only computer we had was about thirty-five years old and none of us had ever studied moviemaking. We didn't stand a chance.

Daisy waved her sign-up sheet in the air and a rush of people headed for the salmon stall she was teetering on. My heart raced. I couldn't let all these people sign up to Daisy's movie!

I leapt on to the nearest crab stall, my trainers crunching over the ice that was keeping the catch fresh. Kai whistled for the crowd's attention and Fabien dragged Daisy's microphone over to me.

I felt the whole town's eyes burning into my skin, waiting.

"We're not amateurs!" I yelled, after sucking in a massive breath of courage.

The crowd quietened. I took another deep breath, and tried not to mess up. My tummy fluttered with nerves. It was a bit scary talking to so many people all at once, even though I knew most of them. I tried to picture them wearing donkey costumes and it made me feel a bit better.

Daisy raised an eyebrow. "You've made a movie before?"

"No, but we know what we're doing," I lied. "Good movies aren't all about fancy camera angles and lighting. The important thing is the story, and we have the best one. We're going to show how wonderful Wishnook and *most* of you already are."

"You're going to embarrass us all!" yelled Daisy. "Even fewer people will want to come here!"

"Can I be in the movie? I can burp the alphabet in French," said Brice, a boy at the back.

Before I could ask how that was different to burping it in English, let alone why I'd want to record him doing it, Farmer McAndrew piped up from a few rows away. "My cows would be brilliant in a movie. They're very talented, you know. Betsy can make three litres of milk in under thirty seconds, if you hum her the theme tune to *Thunderbirds.*"

"Wow, that's … a special gift," I said. "Anyway, if you want to be in our movie rather than Daisy's, you can sign up with us instead."

Some of the crowd moved away from Daisy's clipboard and towards the crab stall I was balanced on. I watched them part down the middle, as everyone picked a side. Mum smiled proudly at me and joined the queue that was forming at my feet, and Dad dithered for a second before going towards Daisy. I couldn't believe he was on the side of the development!

Mum shook her head when she spotted Dad, then grabbed a whelk from somebody's cup, and threw it at his shoulder to get his attention. It bounced off his T-shirt, soared into the air and pinged Declan the butcher on the nose. He sneezed with shock, picked it up from the floor and threw it back at Mum.

Suddenly another whelk went flying, though I couldn't see who had thrown it. There was a scream in the crowd as Edna ducked out of its path then grabbed a handful of her own and launched them skywards. Before I knew it, the air was full of whelks, seaweed, sprats and little chips of ice. It was a full-on food fight.

Gulls and dogs tore around the harbour, hoovering up the food as it bounced off people and tumbled to the floor. There were more screams and yells, and I saw Mrs Percy threaten her husband with a trout. Jim, one of the fishermen, started flinging invoices at people for the sprats they'd nicked. It was chaos. Daisy's eyes glinted happily, as she filmed the whole debacle.

I took cover under the crab stall and peeked out from beneath the tablecloth. Somebody had made it through the war zone and was scribbling their name at the top of Daisy's list, ponytail bobbing as they wrote. I gasped in shock when I realised who it was.

Margot.

"You can't join her side!" I yelled, springing up and ducking a lemon wedge.

Margot turned round guiltily. "I'm sorry, Luna, but you know I think the development is a good idea."

I couldn't believe it. I'd thought Margot had been coming round to our side, but she had betrayed us instead. For the first time in our lives we were properly on different teams.

CHAPTER

SEVEN

I convinced Mum and Dad to take me straight back to the mainland next morning so I could record the auditions for Kai's play. My plan was to spend the day focusing on how artistic and full of culture the town was. I just hoped some of the people auditioning could actually act.

Mrs Percy, our school teacher, was first up. I found the switch for the Wishnook Community Theatre's spotlights, blew the dust off and flipped it. Mrs Percy screamed from the stage.

"Aliens!"

"It's not aliens; it's just the light," said Kai.

"Oh…" she replied. "Yes, I knew that."

Fabien stood on tiptoes and dusted some blusher on to her cheeks. According to Mrs Percy's CV, she actually had a drama degree and had played a coma patient in not just one but *three* episodes of *Casualty*.

"Lovely," said Fabien, stepping back. Mrs Percy's cheeks now glowed like *she* was an alien.

Fabien, Kai and I took our seats in front of the stage while Mrs Percy perused the script. I looked at the door and wondered what Margot was up to. She'd come to the mainland with us but had disappeared as soon as we docked. I bet she was with Daisy somewhere, begging to be recorded for the Other Movie. My feet tapped with annoyance at the thought.

Mrs Percy cleared her throat and started reciting *she sells seashells on the seashore* at varying speeds, as a vocal warm-up. Kai glanced at his watch. Fabien picked his nose nonchalantly and I readied our camera.

"We do have other people waiting..." prompted Kai.

Mrs Percy raised her script to her smudged glasses. "These things can't be rushed," she muttered.

She read through the script again, then stood on the X in the middle of the stage to start her audition.

"But, Mum, I want to be a footballer!" she whinged in character. "Why do I have to be an accountant?"

I stared at Kai. "I thought your play was about space..."

"Yeah, I went in a slightly different direction and changed it to football," he said, and then stood up. "Mrs Percy, you're meant to be auditioning for the part of Jay's grandmother, not the main character…"

"Yes, well, I thought my experience made me more suitable for the lead," she said.

"But Jay is supposed to be twelve…" said Kai.

"I know," replied Mrs Percy, who was at least sixty. "Just lower the lighting a bit."

I turned the spotlight off so we could barely see her, and Mrs Percy performed the rest of the audition in the dark. To be fair she did sound quite convincing when you couldn't see her grey hair and permanently exhausted expression. I switched the camera on to night mode to make sure we caught the whole thing. It wasn't the worst audition I'd ever seen, but it definitely wasn't the best.

At the end of it Fabien scrambled back on to the stage and handed Mrs Percy a sticker, which said *Good job*. Then he ushered her off the stage, went to the door and shouted, "Next!" at the top of his lungs.

"Did I get it?" asked Mrs Percy, as she was herded out.

"We'll call you," replied Fabien. Then we all shook our heads at each other, and I crossed her name off the list.

Next up was Brice, the boy who Margot had had a crush on last year until she'd discovered he preferred cars to aeroplanes.

"It just doesn't make sense!" she would often say, still trying to process the shock almost a year later. "Cars are just so small, and slow, and hardly any have fully functioning kitchens."

"No cars have kitchens…" I'd tell her.

Fabien poked me in the ribs and I stopped daydreaming about when Margot and I had been friends and focused on Brice again. It looked like he'd already started his audition, also for the part of Jay, although it was kind of hard to tell.

"Football's the only thing I love," he said in a tone that made me think of Eeyore. "Just give me a chance," he droned.

Kai and I exchanged pained looks, and I held up my hand. "Thanks, that's great."

"Don't you want to see me kick a football?" asked Brice.

"Um…" I replied.

"No," said Fabien.

Ignoring us, Brice lined himself up with the

football on the stage floor, swung back his leg and booted it as hard as he could. The ball popped into the sky, cracked a spotlight, ricocheted on to Fabien's head, then bounced off and smacked Kai square in the face.

"Oops. Soz," said Brice.

I checked both Fabien and Kai were still alive, directed Brice to the exit and wrote *set design* next to his name. Then I scribbled it out, thinking he might be even more dangerous with a hammer. Maybe he could hand out ice creams during the interval or something?

"This is terrible," I said. "We're going to need better stuff than this for our movie. The judge will tell them to demolish everything within ten miles at this rate."

"It'll get better," said Kai hopefully.

"My goats can act," Fabien added.

The next person to audition was Frank. He was part of a local band called The Rocking Pensioners, who'd played at our festival last year. He was older than Mrs Percy, although nobody quite knew *how* old. Rumour had it even Frank couldn't pinpoint the exact decade.

"Let me guess, you're auditioning for the part

of Jay?" said Kai.

"No, don't be silly, I'm far too old to play a twelve-year-old," replied Frank.

Kai, Fabien and I all sighed with relief.

"I'm auditioning to play Harry, Jay's big brother," said Frank.

"But he's meant to be fifteen!" cried Kai.

I dimmed the lights again. At this rate all the characters would need to wear head torches just to make sure they didn't fall off the stage. I supposed at least the audience could have glow sticks. We'd just call the whole thing a special effect.

Frank was surprisingly quite good during the odd glimpses that I got of him through the gloom. He couldn't kick the ball, but he did sing a football chant while halfway up a ladder, waving a Celtic scarf.

"What do you think?" I whispered to the others.

"He's a good singer," said Fabien. "Shame about the wrinkles."

"The character's supposed to support Rangers..." replied Kai.

Frank leaned back on his ladder. "You'll have to change that. Celtic are the best!"

Fabien pointed his finger at Frank. "You're hired!"

"Yippee!" said Frank, zipping down the ladder and then clutching his back in agony. "I'm OK. I'm OK."

"Save me," muttered Kai.

"Told you," I whispered back.

I led Frank towards the door. He might have been about sixty years too old, but at least we'd cast one character for Kai's play. Now we just had to find another nine. At this rate we'd have them all by Christmas.

I eased Frank out of the door and blinked in the blinding sunshine. There was a scuffling sound and I caught a whiff of familiar strawberry-scented shampoo. My eyes adjusted to the light and I looked in the direction that the noise had come from. Backing away, with a camera in one hand and a walkie-talkie in the other, was Margot.

"What are *you* doing here?" I said, stepping outside to confront her.

The walkie-talkie buzzed in her hand. "Abort mission, abort mission!" it crackled.

"Is that *Daisy*?"

Margot stuffed the walkie-talkie in her pocket,

but it was too late. I rushed towards her and tried to look at the camera she was holding. The lens twinkled in the light before she crammed the cap over it.

I knew the camera didn't belong to Margot. For a start she'd never mentioned it before, and for another thing this one was huge and probably cost more than our whole year's pocket money combined.

A voice crackled on the radio again, and then I realised exactly what was going on. Margot had been sent to spy on us!

"I haven't!" said Margot, when I accused her.

"Prove it!" I said, grabbing the camera, and pressing the playback button.

Margot lunged at the camera and we squabbled over it as the footage played. I elbowed Margot away, and she elbowed me back. Frank just rolled his eyes at us, and clicked down the hill with his dodgy knees.

I tried to hold the camera still enough to see the footage. There was Mrs Percy walking into the theatre for her audition, and then a shot of Margot's shoes. She must have been loitering in the dark at the back, because she seemed to have recorded the whole of the audition.

"You *have* been spying!" I said. "How much did Daisy pay you?"

"It's not spying," replied Margot. "It's just research for our movie."

"*Our* movie?"

Margot flushed. "Yes… I'm producing it with Daisy."

"You're doing WHAT?"

It was one thing knowing that Margot wanted to be *in* Daisy's movie, but it was quite another for her to actually help record it. She'd not just picked sides; she *was* the other side.

"I can't believe you're helping Daisy instead of us," I yelled. "Worse, you were spying!"

"It was *research*," said Margot again.

I turned on my heels.

This was war.

CHAPTER

EIGHT

Margot and I ate lunch back at the island in silence.

I finally cracked, unable to bear it any more. "I can't believe you're trying to destroy our town."

"It's *you* who's trying to destroy it," said Margot.

I poked my food angrily, trying to work out if it had once been bacon or eggs.

Margot downed a glass of orange juice, presumably to wash the plastic taste of lunch away. "I'm going to help Dad set up this afternoon's summer school."

"Traitor!" I yelled after her.

"Eat your eggs!" she yelled back.

"It's bacon!" I called.

"Actually it's rice," said Mum, popping up outside the kitchen window and passing her coffee mug through the opening.

The tin coffee mug dropped into the sink with a clatter, and Mum disappeared to barbecue a nice lunch for the yoga guests. I abandoned my own food and felt around for the camera in my pocket. I was going to record the dolphins, even though they weren't on my itinerary for the day. There were only nine days left before the court case and we desperately needed more scenes for the movie. Besides, if a pod of dolphins couldn't save our town from demolition, nothing could.

I was almost at the door when it burst open in my face, and Fabien ran at me in a panic.

"What's happened? Did one of the yoga guests chase your goats again?" I asked.

"No, come and look!" he said, and then disappeared in a flash.

I sighed and followed Fabien into the living room. Knowing him, it would be something thoroughly uninteresting and useless, like a woollen lampshade, or a new set of knitting needles he was giving a whirl.

Strangely there weren't any knitted lampshades, or needles, or even balls of yarn in sight. The living room looked exactly like it always did: dull and dusty, with cobwebs that suggested at least a dozen spiders were languishing somewhere nearby.

"OK, what exactly am I looking at?" I asked him.

As I said this, a scraggly old cat strolled out from behind the sofa, sat down near my feet and licked its leg.

I screamed in surprise and the cat leapt up, ran across the room and darted under a cabinet. Was I imagining things? Was that really a cat? I wondered if I'd swallowed too much seawater on the boat and got sick. An annoyed hiss came from under the cabinet, which certainly sounded real.

I turned to Fabien. "Where did you get a cat from?"

"It's not mine!" said Fabien, lying on his tummy and trying to fish it out from under the cabinet.

The cat hissed louder and Fabien backed away. If it wasn't his cat, then what was it doing on our island? Had it swum there? Did cats like water? Perhaps somebody was smuggling them here. It seemed the only logical explanation.

Mum came into the living room and eyed us suspiciously. "What's going on?" she asked.

At the sound of her voice the cat slunk out from under the cabinet, pranced across the room and wrapped itself round Mum's leg. She scooped it up and rocked it gently.

"It's *your* cat?" I said.

"Yes. I'm trying out something new: yoga with cats," she said.

"What?" I said, completely confused. "You

mean you're teaching yoga to cats now?"

"No, don't be ridiculous," scoffed Mum. "I'm teaching yoga *with* cats, setting a new trend. People get a double whammy of relaxation, by doing yoga and petting a cat at the same time."

As she said this, the latest group of yoga guests charged into the room, ready for their first afternoon on our island. The lady at the front of the group squeaked excitedly, a bit like Fabien did whenever he saw one of his goats, and reached out to pet the kitty. It arched its back and hissed at her.

"Very relaxing," I said, as the cat tried to claw the lady's eyes out.

I left Mum, Hellcat and the yoga guests to it, and sneaked outside with Fabien. If we made a run for it now, maybe I could escape Dad's summer school.

"Luna, Fabien!" called Dad from over by his shed.

I stopped in my tracks and groaned.

"It's time for today's lesson," he said. "Step into my creativity portal."

"Your what?" asked Fabien.

"His shed," I mumbled, then dragged my feet

towards him. "Please tell me today's lesson isn't whittling," I pleaded.

Dad beamed. "Yes, today we whittle!" He clicked his fingers and heels at the same time, like he was in a dreadful old musical.

I wanted to protest more, but then thought it would actually be a brilliant scene for our movie, and another way to show how artistic Wishnook was, so it did kind of fit my itinerary.

Dad ushered me into his shed. It was starting to lose its fresh wood smell now and was taking on a whiff of old socks. The windows fizzed with crickets and crane flies. I assumed they were looking for an escape from the sea of wooden birds, which were now piled ankle high.

Margot was already waiting for us at a bench. I sat opposite her and felt a huge surge of jealousy that Kai and the other kids hadn't been forced to come this time.

I got out my camera and Margot grabbed something from her backpack. It was Daisy's big expensive camera.

"What are you doing?" I asked her.

"Recording the whittling," replied Margot.

"But *I'm* recording the whittling," I said, turning

on my camera. It was half the size of Margot's and significantly more dented.

"Mine's got a times sixty zoom," said Margot. "And Daisy's ordered a GoPro off eBay."

"Well, mine's got... Well, it's just better," I said.

I plonked the camera on the shelf with a huff, angled it so everyone was in view and then drove my chisel into my block of wood. A massive chip flew off and landed in my hair, alongside the bits of hay and leaves that were already embedded there.

Dad grabbed my chisel off me and lurched into a twenty-minute safety introduction. Then he demonstrated a few whittling basics and handed our tools back over to us. I glared at Margot, then flew at my project like a falcon. I had no idea what I was making, but my hands struck the wood so hard I accidentally chiselled the thing into two separate pieces.

Margot drove the chisel at her block of wood equally quickly. I leaned forward and sped up, determined to finish my sculpture before she did. I needed to be better at whittling than Margot. I needed to show her that I was just as clever and talented as she was and that I meant business.

When I was almost finished, Fabien peered at my project and squeaked. "You've made a snowman!" he said, all congratulatory, as I balanced the pieces on top of each other.

"Um … yes," I replied, not telling him it was supposed to be a donkey.

Margot, clearly distracted by my accidental triumph, struck her driftwood too hard and sent a massive splinter towards her forehead. She winced and sprang to her feet, while Dad took a pair of tweezers from his first-aid kit. In the end it took an industrial pair of pliers to dislodge it.

I took the opportunity to record a close-up of Dad's seagulls, while Margot was busy observing the damage to her skin and Fabien continued to whittle what I suspected was a goat figurine. He looked extraordinarily happy, tongue stuck out, humming along to himself.

"Here, film my latest work," said Dad, and he beckoned me over to a workbench behind him, which had a tablecloth draped over it.

I pointed the camera at the workbench, hoping whatever was underneath the cloth would be good. We had to show the judge that Wishnook was full of extraordinary people like artists, bakers, farmers and fishers. Maybe Dad had made something really spectacular that would impress them.

Dad pulled back the cloth and I nearly dropped the camera. On the table was an array of different-shaped, beautifully whittled poos.

"What do you think?" he said, lifting one towards me. It was long and pointy and shiny.

"Why have you whittled a poo?!" I screamed.

Dad looked taken aback. "It's not a poo – it's an iced bun."

Margot came over to inspect the object with her own camera. "Um … that's a poo, Dad."

"No it's not!" he exclaimed. "Don't be ridiculous."

I picked up something swirly from the table. "What about this one?"

"That's a cupcake with icing," he said.

"Are you sure? Because it doesn't look like it…" I replied.

"Of course I'm sure. I'm whittling a patisserie!" he answered.

Margot and I both raised our eyebrows, and for a second I almost forgot we weren't speaking. I couldn't include this in our movie. We were supposed to be showing the appeal judge that Wishnook was perfect, and Dad's pootisserie was about as far from that as you could get. The day was a complete washout, and we didn't have many of them left to waste.

CHAPTER

NINE

"What should we record today?" I asked Kai the next day, after I'd found him in The Wig and Pen. Mum had taken the yoga guests on a tour around the mainland, though there wasn't much to see these days.

"I dunno. Let's just try to do as much as we can. There's only just over a week now, right?" he said.

"Eight days," I replied, which sounded like quite a long time, but there was still so much to do. For one we had to teach ourselves how to smoosh all the clips together on Kai's computer and then figure out how to add things like special effects. We hadn't even downloaded the movie-editing program yet.

"Film me!" cried Kai's mum from behind the bar. "I'm making a haggis for Declan's birthday."

I glanced at Kai. "What's a haggis again?"

"It's what you ate on Burns Night, remember?" he said. "Best not to ask what it's made of, though."

I thought about our list of things that I wanted to film and food was definitely on it. While Kai went to distract Margot and Fabien, I slipped behind the bar and followed Heidi into the kitchen with our camera. A horrible smell smacked me in the face when she opened the door. It was like mouldy cheese festering in a pigsty. Across the room a red bucket stuck out of the metal sink.

"Is *this* what I ate on Burns Night?" I asked Heidi, peering inside. It was filled with some sort of slimy grey meat.

"Of course," she replied. "Obviously you ate the finished version, though – cooked offal stuffed inside a sheep's stomach."

My cheeks bulged and for a moment I thought I was actually going to be sick. Offal was things like kidneys and hearts. I held the camera and filmed it at arm's length. Maybe we could make it look prettier when we edited it.

Fabien's singing drifted towards the kitchen and the hairs on my arm stuck up. I couldn't let him see the sheep offal. He didn't even agree with people eating lamb chops. If he found out about this, he'd never leave our island again.

I threw myself in front of the offal and shielded it from view.

"Wow, what's that weird smell?" asked Fabien.

Kai hurried in after him, panting. "Margot's on the phone to Daisy. I didn't hear much, but it sounds like she's coming over to film too."

Heidi wiped her hands on her apron. "Two film crews in my kitchen! What a day!"

Fabien crept forward, craning his neck to see what I was hiding. I found a cupcake on the side and threw it at him as a distraction, but he caught it without looking and inched closer and closer.

"What's in there?" he asked. "What are you hiding?"

"Nothing!" I said.

"Mutton offal," said Heidi.

Fabien's face turned pale. "Mutton ... that's sheep!" he yelled.

"Yes, it's traditional," replied Heidi.

"You can't cook a sheep!" he shouted.

"Mutton," corrected Heidi.

Margot poked her head round the door. "What's going on? What are you doing?"

"Kai's mum is cooking sheep!" yelled Fabien.

"Mutton!" said Heidi again.

Margot came into the room and peered at the offal. "Oh, haggis! Can I have some?"

Fabien's face turned red and he lunged for the bucket. Startled, Heidi stumbled backwards, and Fabien's little hands wrapped round the bucket's handle. He tore off with it in a flash and I raced after him, with Margot, Heidi and Kai at our heels.

I chased Fabien all the way across the harbour towards the sea.

"Wait, what are you doing?" I yelled at him.

Fabien screeched to a halt at the edge of the water and dangled the bucket above it. Behind us, Heidi panted and held out her arms.

"Now, don't do anything hasty," she said, as Fabien dangled the offal perilously close to the water's surface.

"You can't eat sheep," he told her again. "They have feelings."

"OK, I promise I'll never make another haggis again … after this one," said Heidi, taking the tiniest of tiny steps towards him.

Kai looked worried. "But, Mum, the old people like it."

"Monsters!" yelled Fabien.

I lowered the camera and reached out towards Fabien to try to pull him back to sanity, but it was too late. He turned the bucket upside down and tipped the offal into the water. The slimy grey lumps rained down into the sea. I peered over the edge and saw a flurry of fish dancing around them.

"I now declare this a lamb-and-mutton-eating-free town!" announced Fabien, swilling the bucket out in the sea.

Kai tensed. "What are we supposed to stuff our haggis with now?" he huffed.

Margot stepped between Kai and Fabien, as if worried there might be a punch-up. "Mushrooms would work very well, perhaps in a savoury pancake casing."

I blinked at her. "When did you become Jamie Oliver?"

"When Mum asked me to look up some recipes the other day. Apparently the yoga people didn't fancy spam paella," she replied.

"Who'd have guessed?" I muttered.

I watched the offal sink to the depths of the sea. At least we'd not filmed the whole debacle.

There was a noise behind us and I turned round to find Daisy Gifford with her camera. The recording light was on, and the lens was pointing directly at us.

"Keep going – this is gold!" she called.

"You can't put this in your movie!" I said.

Daisy's camera zoomed further into my face. I grabbed the offal bucket and hid my face behind it, trying not to breathe.

She was going to make Wishnook look like a laughing stock. The planning judge would be practically begging Gold Rush Properties to come and fix us. This was a disaster.

CHAPTER

TEN

"Where are you off to?" asked Dad, who had come to pick us all up.

"I've just got something to do," I replied.

"Well, don't be too long," he said, but Kai, Fabien and I were already halfway across the harbour.

It had taken Fabien an hour to calm down after the offal incident. Mum kept telling him to apologise, but he refused until Heidi agreed to put at least three vegan meals on the menu. Even then I was sure his fingers were crossed when he muttered sorry.

I didn't want to return to the island empty-handed. We needed to find something else to film, and this time we couldn't let it go wrong.

"Let's interview Declan at the butcher's," whispered Kai.

"That's a great idea," I said, though I couldn't remember whose movie Declan had signed up for. We needed the butcher's shop in ours, though. It was the most popular shop in town, even though it was half empty most days. Hopefully we'd be able to talk him round if he was on Daisy's side. We just needed to stop Fabien labelling the lamb chops with *Warning: inedible!* stickers.

I paused when we reached the road and noticed Margot following us. She bent down and pretended to examine her shoes. I tutted. She was such a bad spy.

"What are you doing?" I asked her.

"Nothing..." she said.

"Are you following us again?"

Margot shook her head in denial. "I don't know what you mean. I'm just going for a walk."

"You don't walk anywhere unless you're forced," I replied. "You always say if the universe wanted us to walk places it wouldn't have invented the four forces of flight."

"Lift, thrust, drag and weight," said Margot dreamily.

Fabien tugged on my arm. "Come on, Luna. Dad said we don't have long."

I followed him across the road, and, when I glanced back, Margot was gone.

Kai and I watched Fabien cautiously as we entered the butcher's. The little bell tinkled above our heads. Declan the butcher glanced up from the lamb leg he was marinating, jumped and threw a tea towel over it. Fabien assessed the cabinets, and seemed pleased to see it was mostly fake grass. Luckily Declan must still have been setting up for the day.

"We wondered if we could film you for our movie?" I asked, prodding the camera in his face.

"I've already done an interview with your sister," he said. "Obviously I said Wishnook Vegas is a brilliant idea, and that people should buy my bacon," he replied.

I wasn't sure how those things were related. I also couldn't believe Margot and Daisy had got to Declan before us! They were like ninja moviemakers.

Kai examined the glass counter. "That is a LOVELY gammon joint. I reckon it would look great on our camera. It's got a special food setting."

"Has it?" whispered Fabien.

I shrugged.

Declan regarded the gammon joint with a look of unconditional love. "It really is a smasher. Well, I don't suppose being in two movies would hurt. There's no such thing as bad publicity, as they say."

I pressed record on the camera. To my surprise, *food mode* flashed up on the display when it focused on the gammon joint. It hadn't done that earlier with the offal, but I could see why it wouldn't have thought that was food. It made the gammon look a bit slimy and inedible. I switched it to the beautify setting and the joint gleamed like a gemstone, or at the very least some sort of alien rock. Either way, it was an improvement.

Declan lofted the gammon joint in the air. "Get its good side!" he said, rotating it 180 degrees.

I zoomed in. "Can you tell us about your shop, and why you love living in Wishnook?"

"That's easy," he replied. "My shop is the Harrods of Wishnook, only cheaper, and I don't sell shoes. And the people here know the value of a good slice of black pudding. That's why I love Wishnook."

"But Gold Rush Properties might not," I said. "All their guests are going to be loaded. Posh people don't eat black pudding."

"What is that?" asked Fabien.

"It's pigs' blo—" began the butcher, but I shushed him.

"Something gross that old people eat at breakfast time," I replied.

"And the resort is going to have its own

restaurants and chefs. They won't need to go to a butcher," said Kai.

Declan rocked his food protectively. "The hotel will buy all its meat from me."

"Until stage two of their plan, when they open up a shopping mall and they start shopping at Waitrose," I said.

Declan looked worried, but then shrugged it off and lifted a chain of sausages from his cabinet like it was a snake. He angled his face in front of the camera and started talking loudly about all the herbs and spices he'd used, and how he'd learned to tie sausages from his uncle, who was a plumber. I tuned out.

"Thanks, I think that's all we need," I said, coming back to my senses and backing away.

"Are you sure? I could give you a guided tour of the kitchen. I've just got a new mixer for my handmade stuffing."

Kai and Fabien backed away with me. "No, what we've got is already great," said Kai. "You'll be the star of the whole movie."

Declan's earlobes blushed beneath his hat, as we beat a retreat to the pavement.

The next person on our list to film was Mayor

Oddway, because obviously we needed the mayor of Wishnook in our movie. We set off down the high street towards his office, which was also the local police station and a solicitor's office about twice a year. Before we got there, though, Mike the mechanic zoomed down the road in his ice-cream van.

He'd bought it last year to turn into a camper, and we'd borrowed it off him to sell ice creams at our festival. Turned out Mike had liked them so much that he'd kept the van as it was, so he could eat frozen lollies in between car MOTs.

"Would you like to film the van?" he called.

"I thought you were on Margot's side?" I said.

"Yes, but they wouldn't film the van. Daisy's lactose intolerant and said the smell of Mr Whippies gives her hives," he told me.

I got my camera out again quickly, and Mike did a wheel spin, showing off. He turned on the music and the sweet ice-cream melody tinkled out of the speaker. I laughed as Mike waved out of the window and parked the van so his face was perfectly in shot.

"Another diva," muttered Kai.

Having heard the ice-cream tune, Mr Percy

came running down the hill with a soggy wafer cone in his hand. "Oi, this is my patch! We agreed you wouldn't sell ice creams on the street!" he yelled.

"He's just showing us the van for our movie," I said, trying to avoid an argument.

Mr Percy snorted. "Oh, he's showing off all right. He doesn't even have any ice cream in that van; it's all for show! You should film me and my stall."

Mike cut the engine. "You mean your wallpaper table."

"How dare you!" shouted Mr Percy, and he waved his ice-cream cone at Mike threateningly.

Mike hopped out of the van, reached through the window and grabbed a chocolate flake. The pair stared at each other, wafer and flake raised like swords. Kai stepped between them.

"Look, nobody wants any trouble," he said. "We can record you both; it's fine."

"You can't film that rusty old thing," said Mr Percy. "It'll give a bad name to the ice-cream industry."

"Right, that's it!" replied Mike, and he lunged at Mr Percy with the chocolate flake.

Mr Percy fought back, deflecting the flake with his ice-cream cone, like they were fencing. I carried on recording, because I wasn't really sure what else to do. Fabien stepped behind me, shielding himself from the fight.

I tensed as Mike reached back into his van and pulled out a bottle of chocolate sauce. Mr Percy, having seen what was happening, reached into his pocket and grabbed a container of sprinkles.

"Don't do it," said Kai, backing out of their way.

The pair glared at each other, fingers ready to unleash the confectionary. It was like a low-budget Western.

Just then, Mrs Percy hurried out of the charity shop and yelled at them. "Not again! You're like kids, the pair of you." Then she turned to us and said, "No offence."

Mr Percy and Mike lowered their chocolate sauce and sprinkles.

"Say sorry," she demanded.

The pair folded their arms and looked everywhere apart from at each other.

"Sorry," mumbled Mike.

"Sorry," muttered Mr Percy.

Kai edged back over to me and let out a low

whistle. "You'd never believe they were best mates until this whole development thing started. It's all because they're on different sides that they're like this."

I really hoped our movie could bring them back together. If not, Mike and Mr Percy might never talk to each other again.

CHAPTER

ELEVEN

Luckily we found Mayor Oddway at his desk, working on the appeal paperwork for the court case. I peeped over and tried to get a good look. The Gold Rush plans were even more terrifying up close. The resort was so huge that there were two helicopter pads and a model Eiffel Tower on one of the golf courses. Looking at the map, it dwarfed Wishnook and everybody in it, and a dastardly road cut right through the town like an earthquake. I hated to think how bad things would look if they built their shopping mall too. Where would all the badgers go?

Mayor Oddway cleared all the things off his desk, gave his hair a brush and hung his gold chains round his neck.

"Do you want to do a soundcheck?" he asked.

"No, I think we're OK," said Kai, and he started asking Mayor Oddway about why the resort was such a bad idea.

"There are good developers and bad developers. Gold Rush Properties are the bad kind. All they care about is making money. They won't leave any home for the wildlife, and I'm afraid we'll be trampled on too. Anyone who doesn't fit in with their plans will be forced out.

I've seen them do it to businesses before," he said.

"How could Margot support all this?" I just didn't understand it.

"Our town isn't perfect, and your sister knows that. There's little money here; no opportunities for you young people. I guess she thinks the resort will solve all our problems, like a lot of the town do. They think we'll benefit from the extra visitors, rather than be driven out."

"So who's right?" asked Fabien.

"I think we are," said Mayor Oddway. "But half the town, including Margot and Daisy, think they are."

Kai let out a long whistle. "That's confusing," he said.

Fabien shook his head. "So if Margot and Daisy think they're right, and if *we* think *we're* right, then what if neither of us are?"

"People have to pick a side, though," said Mayor Oddway.

"Why? Can't the Gold Rush people just build a *little* golf course and a *little* hotel? Then everyone will be happy," said Fabien.

"It doesn't work like that," said Mayor Oddway.

"Gold Rush Properties will never agree to build something smaller, because it will make them less money."

"What if we could convince them to?" asked Fabien.

"Some people would still be unhappy, even with a little golf course," said Mayor Oddway. "It's just the way things are."

"Well, it's a bit stupid, if you ask me," muttered Fabien, and then he turned to me. "Can we go home now? My goats will want their elevenses."

I stared at Fabien, wondering how he could go from sounding wise to crazy in the space of five seconds.

Seeing the plans up close made me even more scared about Wishnook Vegas but more determined to stop it too. We were going to protect our countryside and the fish market and Mum's yoga business. We wouldn't fail. We couldn't afford to.

CHAPTER

TWELVE

I woke up the next morning with a knot in my tummy. We'd hardly recorded anything that made Wishnook seem wonderful and sparkly. Mostly we'd just caught people being silly and acting ridiculous. I needed to find some scrap of talent in the town or we were finished.

There was no sign of Fabien in the house, so I grabbed my toast to go and marched across the island in search of him. We needed to go back to the mainland that morning and find something worth recording. My plan was to start at the McAndrews' farm and then decide where to go after that.

I spotted a trail of biscuit crumbs and goat droppings disappearing into the woods and started to follow them. Fabien and his herd were nearby; I could sense it.

Sure enough, when I reached the rock pools, I found Fabien there, bent over the water with a net in one hand and a packet of ginger nuts in the other.

"Are you fishing?" I asked.

"No, collecting barnacles for the goats," replied Fabien. He crumbled some biscuit into the water and poked something with his stick. "Excellent bait, ginger nuts."

I explained to him my plan for the day, and was about to pull him to his feet, when Mum burst out of the trees, panting.

"I need to borrow one of your goats," she said desperately.

"Borrow a goat…?" said Fabien, and I was glad he seemed as confused by this as me.

"Yes," replied Mum. "Cat yoga didn't work out, but then I thought 'goat yoga'!"

It was official; Mum had gone nuts. A year on the island had broken her sanity.

"I'm going to regret asking, but what exactly *is* goat yoga?" I said.

"It's all the rage," said Mum. "I'm so cross that I didn't think of it before."

"Yes, but what *is* it?" I asked.

"It's goats balancing on people doing yoga," said Mum. "You can charge thirty per cent extra for it."

"People will pay thirty per cent extra for one of Fabien's goats to trample on them?"

"Yes. Brilliant, isn't it?" grinned Mum.

Fabien shook his head. "My goats are busy."

"I only need to borrow three of them. Four,

max. And only for two hours a day. Ish," said Mum. "I've already told the yoga guests that it's happening."

"I'm sorry, but I simply can't spare them," replied Fabien.

"I'll buy you a sheep!" yelled Mum slightly hysterically.

"A real sheep? Done!" said Fabien.

He scrabbled to his feet, nipped off behind a tree and returned with a goat, which he deposited in Mum's arms. "Let's go then!"

"Now? You want the sheep … now?" asked Mum.

"Do you want my goat now?" he asked.

"Well … yes…" replied Mum.

"Then I need a sheep now. It's only fair," he said, and set off full of excitement.

I wasn't entirely sure what was happening, but I followed Fabien back to the south beach. Dad and Margot were already in *Lady Agatha*, ready to go and pick up dinner supplies. I climbed on board, ignoring Margot, and tried to explain to Dad that we now also had to buy a sheep from Farmer McAndrew. He raised an eyebrow, but then nodded without questioning it.

We set off and Fabien tugged on the steering wheel, yelling, "Faster, faster, faster!" as we hurtled across the water. I could practically see the sheep dancing behind his eyes.

Maybe we were finally about to record something interesting.

CHAPTER

THIRTEEN

"Come with meeeeeee!" yelled Fabien at the sheep. "I promise you'll love our island."

Farmer McAndrew was stood by the gate, his wellies covered in dried mud. He was shaking his head seriously. Mrs McAndrew leaned on a fence post, trying not to laugh.

Kai jumped over the fence to help Fabien, who was seconds away from being kicked in the head by an angry ewe. Margot looked pale at the sight of Fabien's peril.

"You need the dog," called Farmer McAndrew. "She's in the garden snuffling for figs."

"I'll find her," said Margot, clutching her phone. She was probably hoping to get a signal closer to the house so she could call Daisy.

I followed her back through the farm, partly because I didn't trust her and partly because I wanted to record all the animals. As we neared one of the barns, I caught the scent of burning wood on the breeze. I wondered if Farmer McAndrew was having a bonfire again, but then something danced in the corner of my eye. A wisp of smoke twirled out of the barn door. Margot saw it too, and we both stopped in our tracks.

Flames glinted and flickered behind the glass

window of the barn, like an orange disco ball.

The barn was on fire.

We yelled at the top of our lungs and Mr and Mrs McAndrew raced over. The fire burned blue and orange, and the flames lapped the ceiling beams. I watched them spread along the hay bales, filling the barn. Dad tried to pull the McAndrews away, but they dug their feet into the dry earth and aimed their fire extinguishers at the building. The flames spat and sizzled, and retreated a tiny bit.

Fabien raced over to us, dragging a sheep on a lead. "What happened?"

"It's on fire!" I said.

"What did you do?!" asked Fabien.

"It wasn't us!" replied Margot.

"Maybe it was spontaneous combustion," said Kai. "It can happen to hay sometimes. It's like a chemical reaction or something. Mrs McAndrew explained it once, but I wasn't really listening."

"We should call the fire brigade," said Margot.

She pulled out her mobile but unsurprisingly there still wasn't a signal. Mrs McAndrew patted her pockets, searching for something.

"I can't find the house keys!" she shouted.

"But we need to call the fire brigade!" yelled Mr McAndrew.

"I must have dropped them when I was cleaning the chicken coops," she said.

"Are you sure the house is locked?" asked Kai. "You live in the middle of nowhere."

"I locked it this morning, when I saw people from Gold Rush Properties sneaking around," she said.

"What were they doing here? You don't think this is their fault, do you?" asked Margot.

"I don't know," said Mrs McAndrew, closing her eyes, as if wishing the keys back into her pocket.

"Don't worry. I'll race back to the town and ring the alarm," said Kai.

I glanced back to the barn. The fire extinguishers were helping, but not enough. Dad was still trying to pull Mr McAndrew away, but the farmer elbowed him off and continued to battle the blaze. It looked hopeless.

"I'll come too," said Margot.

"You've caused enough problems," snapped Kai.

Margot looked hurt. "How is this my fault? It wasn't *me* who spontaneously combusted."

For a second I felt bad for Margot. It was one thing for me to be angry with her, but it was different for somebody else to be.

"Watch Fabien and keep him and that sheep away from the fire," I told her. "I'll go with Kai in case he gets a puncture or something. We'll be as quick as we can."

Margot didn't look pleased about being left behind, but before she could protest Fabien started yelling about needing to move his sheep to safety.

Kai and I grabbed our bikes and cycled quicker than we'd ever cycled before. The image of the flames burned in my eyes. It wouldn't be long before the whole barn was gone, and then maybe the rest of the farm. I pedalled harder and harder, pushing my feet towards the ground until my sides felt like they might split apart.

Kai overshot The Wig and Pen, where the nearest phone was, and I slowed in confusion. Where was he going?

He got to the bottom of the high street and skidded to a halt. I slammed on my brakes and crashed into his back wheel. Kai pointed towards the sky. Above us, as high as a lamp post, was a bell. A length of rope was dangling from it. I'd asked Mum what the bell was for once, but she'd just said it was for emergencies. I'd always assumed she meant a tsunami or earthquake, but, thinking about it, I wasn't sure Scotland got many of those.

Kai yanked on the rope and the bell rang out across the high street. Declan poked his head out of the butcher's, a length of half-tied sausages in his hands.

"Fire up at the McAndrews' farm," Kai yelled to him.

"Right. Action stations!" yelled the butcher, throwing the sausages into the gutter and ripping off his apron like Superman. A flock of seagulls descended upon the sausages with a flurry of squawks.

Kai continued to ring the deafeningly loud bell, and soon almost everyone in town had mobilised themselves in the street. A fire engine barrelled down the hill, with Mike the mechanic at the wheel, and Kai's mum inside with a helmet on her head.

"Is this a joke?" I asked Kai. "Where's the proper fire brigade?"

Declan climbed into the fire engine. "We *are* the fire brigade."

"It's a community one," explained Kai. "Wishnook's not big enough to have a full-time one. This is it."

Daisy Gifford motored down the high street in her mini and waved Kai and me into her car. I glared at her and folded my arms. No way was I getting in a car with Daisy. But then I looked around and realised there wasn't anyone else to take us, and cycling would take too long. Reluctantly I opened the door and buckled myself in.

We raced after the fire engine, back towards the McAndrews' farm. I glanced at the front passenger seat, saw Daisy's camera and narrowly resisted the urge to throw it out of the window.

The fire was raging when we arrived back at the farm. I flung off my seat belt and ran towards it. The fire engine pulled up in front of the barn and Declan the butcher unravelled the hose. Edna turned a wheel and water shot out. The force made Declan wobble, and Doug and Mrs Percy had to hold him upright.

The fire spat angrily and ate up the barn's roof. Above us, a bird sped across the thickening sky.

A herd of cows mooed with worry in the distance.

Water spat from the hose. I found Fabien and two sheep near the cow field. On the other side of the fence Margot was herding a flock of ducks across the grass, towards the safety of their coop.

We huddled together and watched the makeshift fire crew tackle the blaze. They took it in turns to hold the hose and aim the frothy water at the roof. The fire continued to burn, but not quite as fiercely as before. Eventually another fire engine turned up, this one with proper firefighters. They aimed their water at the barn and together the two crews started to beat the flames down.

"What are you going to do?" I asked Farmer McAndrew, when the flames finally subsided and we all stood back to survey the damage.

He stood at the edge of the charred barn. "Knock it down and rebuild, I suppose. Luckily it's insured, and everything's replaceable."

One of the proper firefighters came over to talk to the McAndrews. "It seems the blaze might have been started by a lamp being knocked over and switching on."

Who would have been clumsy enough to knock over a lamp? More to the point, why hadn't they bothered to pick it up? Anyone around here would have known that leaving a broken lamp in a barn filled with hay was just asking for trouble. Unless the culprit wasn't from around here...

"It must have been someone from Gold Rush Properties! Mrs McAndrew said they were hanging around earlier," I said. "Do you have CCTV?"

Farmer McAndrew shook his head. "No, but they've been snooping around for weeks, trying to convince us to sell the rest of the farm."

"And you think they knocked over the lamp?" asked Dad.

"It makes sense," said Kai. "They probably did it deliberately."

I turned to Margot and Dad. "Do you see now? They don't care about Wishnook!"

Margot shook her head. "You don't know it was them; you're just guessing. It could have been an animal who knocked over the lamp."

That was it. The final straw. If this didn't make Margot see sense, then nothing would. She was a lost cause.

CHAPTER

FOURTEEN

"Nobody wants to be in our movie," said Kai, when Dad's summer school brought us back to the mainland the next day.

"Why not?!" I said.

The kids from school were all assembled at the harbour with us, waiting with dread to discover what today's lesson was. I couldn't understand why they didn't want to be in our movie. Did they think yesterday's fire had been our fault?

"News of the haggis ban got out, and the whole town's pretty outraged about it," said Kai.

I turned to Harper, the girl nearest to me. "You want to be in our movie, don't you?"

"Mum said I'm not allowed," she said.

Margot, clearly having been listening, came over. "Can you still be in mine?"

"Oh yeah, Mum said that's fine," replied Harper.

"What?!" I said.

This wasn't fair. If nobody would be in our movie, then how could we finish it? We were being hobbled by offal!

"We have to get Fabien to lift the ban," said Kai.

"But he won't," I replied, looking over at Fabien,

who was sat on the bumper of a van knitting a swimming cap.

There was no way Fabien would take back the offal ban in the next week. I'd need six months to talk him round, not six days. We needed a different plan, but the trouble was, I didn't have one. My hands started to sweat. What were we going to do?

Dad climbed on to a lobster trap and explained that he'd organised work experience for us at the fish market. He said it would be a chance to learn all about fish, fishing, selling and how to turn a wallpapering table into a food stall. Basically it was child labour with added clipboards.

"At the start of our next lesson there'll be a pop quiz about what you've learned," he said.

That would be easy, I thought. There were only so many questions he could ask about crabs, whitebait and tablecloths.

Mum, who was waiting to pick up some lobsters for the fancy yoga guests, tutted at him. "Not that there's much point. The market won't be here once Gold Rush Properties get their claws into the town."

"It can be relocated," said Dad.

The stall owners all started yelling in agreement or disagreement, and Mum and Dad went back to ignoring each other.

"Are your parents OK?" asked Kai.

I nodded. "Yeah, they're not always like this. It's just when one of them mentions Wishnook Vegas. Sooner or later Dad will realise he's wrong; Mum will make him."

The market was the quietest I'd ever seen it because it didn't open for another hour. I looked around for the crab-stall owner and helped her carry things out of her van. After that, I helped somebody else arrange a pile of trout on to trays of thick ice. They were fresh and glassy-eyed and really quite disgusting. I shovelled ice over their fins quickly, and vowed never to become a fishmonger.

The market was just about to open when Kai came over to me, looking excited. "Uncle Doug said he'll take us out in his boat to collect his lobster pots. We wanted to film the fishermen, and this is basically the same thing."

"Brilliant! Which boat are we taking?" I asked.

"*Sir Chance-a-lot*," he said, pointing to a boat that had even more holes in it than *Lady Agatha*.

It was a tiny thing, little bigger than a tuna can, but with a motor that wobbled every time the water rippled.

"Why's it called that?" I asked nervously.

"Because you take a chance that it won't sink," said Kai.

I weighed up what would be worse: sinking in the Scottish sea or missing a really good scene for our movie. There wasn't much contest.

"Lead the way," I said, and then beckoned Fabien over.

"We won't actually sink, will we?" he asked.

I looked at Kai and he shuffled uncomfortably. "Um ... no, definitely not."

I reckoned his fingers were crossed behind his back.

"Where's Margot?" I asked, but before anyone could answer I caught a glimpse of her getting on to a nearby boat. There was something glinting in her hand. It was Daisy's camera. She was going to film something.

"What are you doing?" I yelled at her.

Daisy's head popped out from the cabin of Jim's boat, which was the same one Margot was climbing into. "Lobster catching!"

"You can't! That was our idea!" I yelled.

"I know, we overheard!" yelled Daisy.

I glared at Margot. "You can't just nick our idea!"

"We should make this into a competition," said Daisy. "Whoever brings back the biggest lobster wins."

I folded my arms. "That's silly."

Kai looked thoughtful. "Actually it might make quite a good scene for the movie. You know, a bit of drama."

"So we're really having a fishing contest?" I asked.

"A *crustacean* contest," corrected Daisy from afar.

Fabien practically threw himself into *Sir Chance-a-lot*. "Let's go!" he yelled.

I climbed into the rickety old boat and hoped luck really would be on our side.

CHAPTER

FIFTEEN

We headed to a rocky outcrop, where I saw a group of buoys floating on the calm surface. These weren't the type of buoys that kept boats away from the shore but instead had lobster pots attached to them somewhere underneath the waves, marking the spot where the fishermen could find them and pull them up to the surface.

Doug's buoys were red and Jim the fisherman's were blue. I peered overboard and tried to spy the lobster pots beneath the surface, but all I saw was my own wobbly reflection.

Margot's boat drew level with the blue buoys and she lunged at the first one excitedly. The competition was on.

I grabbed one of the red buoys and pulled, completely forgetting I was supposed to be filming it all. Luckily Kai had remembered and turned on the camera. Margot was already on her second pot, but *I* wanted to be the first to retrieve all the lobsters.

I tugged the rope with all my strength, but the lobster pot was heavier than I'd expected. Fabien grabbed my hands to help, and together we heaved the pot to the surface. I glanced inside. Empty!

Doug pulled up the next one and I saw a tiny lobster, which he said we'd have to throw straight back. There were only a few buoys left, so Fabien and I tugged them up one by one with all our might. The pots burst through the surface, and this time there were lobsters inside them.

I glanced over at Margot's boat. Margot was holding a lobster and Daisy was filming her. It looked like they'd retrieved all their pots already. I'd lost the unofficial race to be first.

Then I saw Jim, the fisherman whose boat they'd gone out on, look up from his fishing magazine and freeze.

"You've let all the lobsters out!" he exclaimed to Daisy. "They're all over the deck!"

"Well, we couldn't film them in the pots, could we?" said Daisy.

Jim's face turned white. "Where's Stan?"

"You mean your pet lobster?" said Margot.

"Yes," said Jim. "He's gone!"

Jim was the only fisherman I'd ever heard of who kept a pet lobster in his house. It had started out living in his bath, but eventually he'd made a full-blown aquarium for it. I had no idea why.

"You brought your pet lobster on a lobster-fishing expedition?" asked Margot.

"He comes everywhere with me!" Jim wailed. "Now all the lobsters are everywhere, and I don't know which one is Stan!"

Doug manoeuvred our boat so we were up alongside Jim's and I clambered over to help search for Stan. The boats wobbled as I crossed them, and I nearly did the splits.

I tried to remember what Stan looked like, but my mind drew a blank, other than he was little, black and had a very hard shell that glistened under the sun. I looked at all the lobsters by my feet. They were identical.

Jim lifted each lobster one by one, and inspected them closely.

"You could try calling his name," said Fabien, who'd managed to climb over too.

"He's not a dog," said Margot.

"No, but it might work," said Fabien.

Jim scratched his beard, then knelt down and bellowed, "Stanley!"

Two of the lobsters pinched their claws at him and Jim picked them both up and looked them in the eyes. They seemed utterly identical to me.

"This one's Stan!" he yelled, holding one to the

sky. A seagull dived for it, and Jim hid the lobster under his shirt.

"How do you know?" I asked.

"I can sense it," he replied. "Plus, he's the right size."

I shrugged, and Jim patted the lobster on its head. Fabien peered at the crustacean to get a better look, and I winced as the lobster flexed its claw and pinched Fabien on the nose. He howled and hopped away.

"Oh, that's definitely Stan," I said, thinking back to last year, when Jim's lobster had attached itself to Fabien's nose in exactly the same way.

With Stan safely rounded up, I hopped back into Doug's boat and started weighing our own lobsters. There was a size chart stuck to the counter; if a lobster was too small, we had to throw it back. I made a note of all the weights and then Fabien arranged the lobsters in size order. One of them must have weighed the same as a small car. I popped him carefully inside a basket. Surely he'd be bigger than any of Daisy's catch.

In the other boat Margot plonked Stan the lobster on the scales. He was a plump thing, and looked much bigger than any of ours.

"Stan doesn't count – you can't weigh him! It has to be a lobster you've caught," I called.

"The rules don't say that," replied Daisy.

Jim plucked Stan away from Margot and cradled him in his arms gently. "They do now. He's been through enough this morning."

Daisy huffed, and she and Margot finished weighing the rest of the lobsters. None of them looked quite as big as Stan, who was clearly well fed. I held my breath and hoped we'd won.

Doug collected up our list of weights and compared them with Margot's list. I tapped my feet nervously.

"We have the biggest lobster," announced Doug, pointing at the whopper I'd put in the basket.

I leapt into the air and whooped. Suddenly Margot threw herself into our boat, arm outstretched for the list. I guessed she wanted to verify the results, but she made the whole thing wobble and she slipped dangerously close to the edge of the boat.

Kai reached out and grabbed her, but his feet skidded like he was on ice. I watched, heart in mouth, as the pair tipped over the side of the boat.

Margot managed to grab on to something and save herself, but Kai slipped out of sight with a splash.

"Kai!" I yelled.

I ran over to the edge of the boat and looked down. Kai bobbed up to the surface in his life jacket, arms flailing, water splashing. I heard him splutter and gasp for air. He must have swallowed some of the water. Fear ran through me.

A wave came up and pushed him away from the boat. I yelled for him again and grabbed a life ring. Another wave rose up and for a moment I lost sight of him.

I kicked off my shoes to jump in, but Margot grabbed me. I tried to shake her off. Did she want him to get pulled away by the waves? Somebody needed to save him!

"It's too dangerous!" yelled Margot.

I managed to elbow Margot away and swung a leg over the edge of the boat. Then, just as I was about to plunge into the water, I caught sight of Kai again. He was battling against the water, trying to get back to us.

"Grab this!" I yelled at him.

I threw the life ring at Kai and he managed to grab hold of it. But a big wave rose up and I saw his grip slip. Somehow he clung on just long enough for Fabien, Doug, Margot and me to pull him back to safety.

I wasn't sure who was shaking more: me or Kai. Margot grabbed a towel and wrapped it round him tightly. It might have been summer, but the sea was bitterly cold this early, like a giant ice bath. He'd probably get hypothermia or at least frostbite.

"Are you all right?" I asked. The thought of losing my best friend was even worse than losing the island.

"The camera," he spluttered. "It's ruined!"

I stared at the camera, which was hanging round Kai's neck. Water poured out of every screw hole and joint. My heart plummeted. It was destroyed.

"It doesn't matter," I said.

"Yes it does," he said. "How can we finish the movie?"

"The most important thing is you're not dead," I said. "No thanks to Margot."

"I didn't mean to slip," she said.

"It's not her fault," said Kai.

I knew she hadn't meant to make him fall, but if she and Daisy hadn't stolen our idea, she wouldn't have been out here and Kai wouldn't have slipped trying to save her. They might not have meant it to happen, but it *was* their fault that Kai had just drunk half a freezing ocean. And it was absolutely their fault our movie was ruined.

CHAPTER

SIXTEEN

"Why is Einstein in the shower again?!" shouted Margot from somewhere inside the bathroom.

"Luna, Margot's trying to banish my goat!" yelled Fabien. "Help!"

I raised my head from my pillow with a sigh and staggered slowly out into the hallway. I'd shut myself in my bedroom as soon as we'd got back from the mainland the day before. Everything seemed totally pointless now the camera was destroyed. I didn't want to see or talk to anyone, especially Margot, but for some annoying reason I couldn't ignore Fabien's plea.

I peered half-heartedly into the bathroom and saw a goat licking a bottle of minty-fresh shampoo. He was wearing Margot's shower cap on his horns, and looked rather proud of it.

Fabien popped up from behind the goat. "Can't you wash outside?" he asked Margot.

"Can't you wash your *goat* outside?" she said.

"No, he prefers it in here," replied Fabien.

I stared at the goat with its damp sudsy fur. "Why are you cleaning Einstein?"

"He rolled over a plate of Vegemite," said Fabien, very matter of fact.

I didn't bother to ask how. This sort of thing

wasn't a strange occurrence where Fabien was concerned.

"But I really need a shower. I still smell from the fish market," said Margot, nudging Einstein towards the plug end of the bath.

"That's a shame," I said, though it wasn't. It served her right for breaking our camera.

"I'm sorry – it was an accident," said Margot again. She'd been saying it on a loop from the other side of my bedroom door for hours.

Fabien grabbed a bottle of Mum's perfume and squirted it in Margot's face. I watched her cough and stumble backwards, and prepared for her to declare war on Fabien and his goat. Instead, she sniffed her pyjamas and raised her eyebrows in surprise.

"That's actually quite nice," she said.

I almost smiled and then felt a pang in my tummy. How could I just give up on Wishnook and on our lives on the island? What had I been doing moping around like it was all over? There were still five days until the appeal. That was long enough to find another camera and record everything again. It would be tight, but it was possible. More than that, we *had* to do it! And it would be ten times better now we kind of knew what we were doing. I could make everything OK again. There was still time.

Suddenly I heard footsteps thudding up the stairs and Kai burst into the bathroom. He doubled over, wheezing, like he'd just been in a race with Usain Bolt.

"What's wrong?" I asked. "What are you doing here? It's not summer school again, is it?"

"No, it's the court case," he gasped. "They've moved it forward to tomorrow!"

I almost fell into the bath with Fabien and Einstein. "WHAT?! That doesn't give us time to fix things!"

"I know. It's all over," replied Kai.

This was a disaster. There wasn't enough time to record our movie, and without that nobody would ever know how brilliant Wishnook was. The judge wouldn't take our side. We were doomed.

CHAPTER

SEVENTEEN

My heart thumped as I sat down on a courtroom chair and waited for the judge. There was a table at the other end of the room, which I guessed was where they'd sit, and a laptop set up ready. My fingers twitched nervously. Any moment now Daisy and Margot's movie would be played for the judge, and everything would be over.

Fabien patted my hand to stop me fidgeting, but Kai's feet started to twitch on the other side of me. Across the aisle, Dad, Daisy and the rest of the "for" people were sat looking equally anxious. Nobody spoke to each other.

I blinked a few times, my eyes stinging with tiredness. My dreams last night had been filled with netted hedges and orange flames. I'd hardly been able to look my donkeys in the eyes when I'd given them breakfast. How could I tell them it had all gone wrong?

The door behind us swung open and a team of suits stomped up the aisle and sat down in a row of chairs at the big table. There were three men, who all looked largely identical, and a woman. I leaned forward and studied them, trying to guess who they were. They each had a briefcase and their jackets seemed to shimmer under the bright lights, like the threads were made of steel or something.

"They must be the Gold Rush people," whispered Kai.

The suits stared straight ahead, ignoring everyone around them. I glanced at Daisy, who was bouncing up and down on her chair, like Fabien did whenever he ate too much chocolate. They must have been like a rock band to her.

"What do you think is in their briefcases?" I whispered to Kai.

He shrugged. "Boring stuff."

The tallest suit took out a massive chunk of paperwork and set it down on the table. I gulped at the size of it. Was that all the "for" arguments? It looked a lot more than Mayor Oddway's bits of paper. Really we didn't have any evidence that Wishnook Vegas would be a bad thing; it was just our gut feeling. I wasn't sure that would stack up against whatever the suits had in front of them.

After what felt like an age, a door at the other end of the room opened and the judge entered. He didn't look much like I'd expected him to, because he didn't have a wig or one of those cloak things, and nobody stood up. For a moment

I wondered if he was just a businessman who'd got lost. His suit didn't look as expensive as the ones the Gold Rush people were wearing, so he obviously wasn't one of them.

"My name's Mr James, and I'm assessing this appeal," he began.

I glanced at Mum, confused. Did he mean he was a newspaper reporter, like Daisy? Why was he making a decision about the development? Mum looked confused too, but then the man went on to explain that he was something to do with the government, so I tried not to worry.

"Now, I'm told that Mayor Oddway has produced a movie in support of this development," said Mr James.

Daisy practically flew off her chair. "No, *I've* made a movie! It's me!"

For the first time since they'd entered, the big-money suits turned round to look at us all. Their eyes landed on Daisy and her face turned a bit pink and flustered. She was definitely star-struck.

"We don't want to submit any video evidence," the smallest suit said, addressing Mr James.

"But my movie's brilliant!" said Daisy, her happy pink cheeks taking on more of an angry red flush.

Mr James scowled at both Daisy and the suit for interrupting his proceedings. "I will take all evidence into account, including the video evidence mentioned."

"Cor, the Gold Rush people don't look happy about that," whispered Kai, and he was right.

Mr James ushered Mayor Oddway to stand up and make his opening argument against the development. I listened carefully as the mayor started talking about all the bad things that would happen if Wishnook Vegas went ahead: the disappearing fields, the homeless animals, the businesses forced to sell up and the loss of the town's culture. Maybe we didn't need our movie after all. Mayor Oddway was doing a good job of making it sound really bad.

The Gold Rush people were asked to make their opening case next, and they began to reel off numbers and use strange words and say things that didn't make any sense to me at all. The only thing I really understood was the word "money", which they said would come pouring into Wishnook and Scotland. Mr James scribbled notes but his face gave nothing away.

My head started to swim as I tried to keep up

with it all, to understand the numbers and jargon. Then finally Mr James signalled for them to sit down and turned his attention to the laptop.

"Thank you for your submissions. I will now consider the video evidence in support of this development," he said.

I sucked in a nervous breath. I wasn't ready for this. I didn't want to see what Daisy and Margot had done. I just wanted to run away.

He pressed a button on the laptop and the movie began to play on the big pull-down screen at the side of the courtroom. It opened with a black-and-white shot of the high street and then cut to the closed-up shops. Sombre music played and Daisy's voice boomed over it all.

"Wishnook is broken. First the tourists disappeared, and then our businesses. The world has changed, but Wishnook has remained in the past. We've been forgotten about, and unless something changes our town is doomed. We need investment. We need development. We need somebody to remind the world that we exist, a reason for people to come here."

The scene cut to Declan the butcher, who was explaining how he hadn't sold nearly as many burgers that summer as he had the year before. He held the burgers aloft, angling them in the light so they shone majestically.

"The tourists used to come in their droves for my special barbecue boxes of burgers and sausages. Now it's hardly worth me making them up," he said. "It's mostly just my cat who eats them, and she haggles the price down something terrible."

Next there was the shot of Fabien emptying his bucket into the sea, with another voice-over from Daisy. "The children are running wild. There's nothing for them to do, so they tip offal into the sea for fun."

Fabien's ears glowed red. "That's not true!"

I shushed him, and now it was *my* turn to hold *his* hand. "Just ignore her," I whispered, but sneaked in a glare at Daisy and Margot for good measure.

There was an interview with Mike the mechanic after that, during which he was sat next to a pile of tyres. More depressing music played, and there was a close-up of his sad eyes fluttering at us all from the screen.

"I haven't serviced a car in weeks," he said. "The last appointment I had was to scrub sick off a seat cover. Things can't go on like this."

Then it cut to the fishing trip. Daisy panned over the lobsters that were spilt over Jim's deck and told the audience about how the seafood was piling up uneaten. She'd spliced in the fish market fight scene for good measure, saying people were just throwing away the food because there was nobody to buy it.

"That's not true either!" yelled Fabien.

Mr James leaned forward. "One more word and I'll have to ask you to leave, young man."

Fabien shrank back into his chair. The Gold Rush people smirked.

There were more moody shots. The tide going out, fish lying in crates, unbought. There were more boarded-up windows, more closed signs on shops. Even the seagulls looked depressed. This wasn't our home. Wishnook was alive and happy and beautiful… But maybe that was just how *I* saw it. Maybe Daisy's movie showed the truth, or at least a kind of truth. Maybe things couldn't survive as they were?

I wanted to close my eyes but forced myself to keep them open. She showed the nets being taken down from the hedgerow and said how

Gold Rush Properties were "committed to the environment". When it came to the fire, she conveniently forgot to mention who'd started it.

Farmer McAndrew stood up. "Pause the movie! It was Gold Rush Properties who burned down my barn. They were seen sneaking about the farm on the morning the fire broke out. They've been trying to force me into selling them the rest of my land for months."

"Nonsense!" somebody yelled.

"Bullies!" said somebody else.

Everyone started shouting and jeering, while Mr James climbed to his feet and demanded silence.

The Gold Rush people reached into their briefcases and clipped microphones to their suits so they could be heard above the racket.

"Those accusations are entirely untrue and actually slanderous," said one of the suits. "We strongly deny all involvement with the unfortunate fire at the McAndrews' farm. Gold Rush Properties is a highly responsible, community-minded developer and we'd never stoop to such tactics."

"What's he going on about?" I whispered to Kai.

"I dunno, it's just kind of waffle," he replied.

But it was waffle Mr James seemed to believe. He nodded at the developers and waved gently at them to sit down.

"Does anyone have any evidence that Gold Rush Properties was behind the fire? I mean real hard evidence," he said.

The crowd finally quietened.

"But we know it was them!" I yelled, unable to keep quiet any longer. "They don't care about anything! They netted the hedgerows knowing it would trap the birds. They covered our beach in washed-up plastic. They're going to build over our home, and steal my mum's yoga customers. They're going to take everything away!"

Mr James shushed me more unkindly than he'd shushed the developers.

"That does not constitute evidence," he replied. "Now, I will ask you all again to be quiet, or I will have to ask you to leave."

Everyone sat down. I stared at the floor miserably, only glancing up to see the end of Daisy's movie. The last shot was of a grey cloud-filled sky. I peeked around the room. Everyone appeared thoroughly miserable, even the "for" people. It made our town seem like the worst place on Earth.

Was it? Had I been completely wrong all this time?

I couldn't look at Margot. The worst thing about it all was she hadn't been entirely wrong in wanting to change the town. Even though their movie had exaggerated stuff, there were little bits of truth hidden in it. Most of the fish did lie unsold at the end of the fish market, though people didn't just throw it across the harbour for the gulls. There wasn't much for kids to do in Wishnook. That's why Dad had started his excruciating summer school. And Declan really *was* sad that he'd hardly sold any sausages that year. I guessed our town wasn't as perfect as I'd thought.

There was more arguing after the movie had finished, though I didn't understand most of what was being said. The people from Gold Rush Properties kept their microphones on and their voices bounced off the walls, deafening us. It made them seem like they were giants.

By the end of the hearing I knew they were invincible.

CHAPTER

EIGHTEEN

My legs were nearly numb by the time the appeal ended.

"I will now go away and consider the arguments, and notify you in writing of the decision," said Mr James. Then he swept out of the room.

I nearly fell off my chair. "Isn't he going to tell us today?" I squeaked.

"Try not to worry," said Mum from her seat in the row ahead.

I wasn't sure I could wait any longer to find out. What would I tell Sunshine and Monty and Moon? If Wishnook Vegas went ahead, and everyone stopped going to Mum's retreats, I wouldn't be able to afford their feed. It was too horrible to bear. I knew now that our town needed saving; I could see that. But I was still sure Wishnook Vegas wasn't the way to do it.

The Gold Rush people stomped down the aisle and out of the courtroom. Everyone else stayed where they were, split down the middle, for and against. I didn't know how we could ever find ourselves on the same side of things again.

One of the speakers on the wall crackled. "We've got it in the bag," said a voice.

Everyone stopped what they were doing and

looked round. Then it dawned on us: the Gold Rush people had left their microphones on!

"We'll have to destroy the movie that interfering old hack made," said the woman's voice.

Daisy shot to her feet. "Interfering?! Old?! A *hack*?!" she cried.

Margot reached out and pulled her back to her seat, shushing her. The Gold Rush people obviously hadn't heard her outburst, because their voices still crackled through the speakers.

"Can you imagine if it was ever published?" said another of the disembodied voices. "It makes all the locals look like complete and utter lunatics, which they are. No wonder the tourists have stopped coming here. Imagine staying above some grubby little pub and buying fatty sausages from that odd butcher."

"Fatty! How dare they?!" exclaimed Declan, and now it was my turn to shush him.

"Not exactly a classy bunch, are they?" sneered the woman's voice. "We'll have to keep the locals from mixing with our sophisticated guests. Better tell Tarquin that we'll need to up security to keep the riff-raff away."

"The sooner we can get to work, the better,"

said one of the men. "We'll just have to buy them off. It shouldn't take much money to make these people change their minds about selling up."

"If not, they'll be easy enough to force out. We'll swallow the land up until they've got nowhere left to go," said one of the other men. "And that island across the sea will be perfect for a theme park."

My blood turned cold. That was *our* island they were talking about! Our island they wanted to dump a theme park on. They wanted to cut down our wood and replace it with twisted pieces of metal and put turnstiles on the beach. I knew they'd come for it after Wishnook. They wanted everything, the whole lot.

"I'm not having that!" said Mum, rolling up her sleeves.

Everyone started to shout. Margot looked green and Daisy wobbled in her seat.

"Wait ... are the microphones still on?" The woman's voice came through the speaker.

Someone swore and there was a buzz, and then silence.

CHAPTER
NINETEEN

I sat, open-mouthed, like the rest of the room. I'd been right after all: Gold Rush Properties wanted to get rid of us. They wanted to destroy Wishnook and replace it with something big and shiny and only for other rich, perfect-looking people. We wouldn't be welcome there any more. That had been the Gold Rush plan from the beginning. They wanted to get rid of us and control everything. We were like ants in a garden to them: annoying, little and unwelcome.

Margot leapt to her feet, tears in her eyes, and charged down the aisle. I hurried after her, wondering what she was going to do. Was she going to go off with the Gold Rush people in their limo? Did she want to help draw up the theme-park plans? I didn't know which side she was on any more. She liked flying, so she'd probably love being halfway up a rollercoaster. Maybe they'd give her a free pass in exchange for helping them out.

I heard everyone stomp after us as I charged through the doors after Margot. The Gold Rush people were already at the other end of the corridor, running with their mic packs trailing. Their shoes clomped on the floor like the feet of a charging rhino.

"Stop!" yelled Margot.

She burst out of the front door after the suits and I stumbled into the daylight after her. Margot took the steps three at a time and caught hold of the woman's jacket. Not a single thread seemed to wrinkle as she tugged it.

The woman turned and shooed Margot away. "Do you mind? This is designer!"

"You can't have our island!" yelled Margot.

"Of course we can, little girl," said the woman. "And I'll be sending my dry-cleaning bill to you."

"We can do anything we want," said one of the men, stopping and turning on us. "We've got money, and in this world money is power. It always wins."

I stood next to Margot and pulled back my shoulders, willing myself to grow taller. "That's not right!"

"Who cares? The world revolves around money, not about what's right and wrong. You'll see that when you grow up," he replied.

"No I won't!" I said, but secretly I was worried.

Was what he said true? Wishnook had run out of money and everything was closing. Maybe they were right. Maybe money *was* the most important thing in the world. But, no, I didn't believe that. It wasn't more important than my donkeys, or Fabien's goats, or the way Margot's eyes lit up whenever she saw a plane. I knew we needed some money, but we didn't need *all* of it. I wouldn't swap Sunshine for all the piles of gold in the world.

"That's not true," said Fabien, catching up. "Mr Billionaire gave us his island for free because he wanted to do something nice. Not all rich people are mean like you."

"Well said, darling," said Mum, who was right behind Fabien.

"Your billionaire is a fool, and he'll end up bankrupt," said the Gold Rush woman.

"He'd still be the happiest old man I've ever met," I said.

The whole town had gathered on the steps behind us now and were shouting out in agreement. Through the middle of them came Daisy, her handbag swinging manically.

"You called me old, and a hack!" she yelled at the suits.

"Your little movie might have been helpful back

there but we can't have anyone else seeing it. Or have you sticking your nose into our business," said one of the men. "You'll be going soon too, Lois Lane, when we buy up your newspaper."

"It's not for sale!" said Daisy.

"Everything's for sale," said the man. "Don't worry. We'll give you enough money to start again, or at least buy a one-way ticket to London, where you'll be out of the way."

"But I supported you! I stood up for Wishnook Vegas," said Daisy.

"And we thank you for it," said the tall man, smirking.

"Me too, and you called my sausages fatty!" yelled Declan.

"Sausages are very old-school, I'm afraid," said the Gold Rush woman. "Our restaurants serve *saucissons*."

"What the blazes is that?" demanded Declan.

"It's sausages, but in French," replied Daisy, and then she turned to the Gold Rush people. "See, I can speak French!"

"*Très bon*," said the woman, and with that they stomped down the remaining steps and sped away in a blacked-out car. Everyone stood, stunned, not knowing what to say. Daisy clutched her pen to her chest, as if terrified they might come back and take it away. Dad shook his head and patted the wooden seagull in his pocket, trying to calm himself.

"I'm sorry, you were right about them," whispered Margot.

"I told you!" I said.

"I know … I know…" she replied, and her face was all squashed up, like a sad frog. "I just thought they weren't as bad as everyone was making out! I thought they'd make things better."

"But they won't. They want us all gone!" I said.

Margot shook her head. "I'm so sorry."

"So are you on our side now?" I asked.

Margot bit her lip. "Yes, of course," she replied after a pause. "We have to stop them. Your movie has to stop them."

I turned to Daisy, whose face was so red it looked like she'd had a fortnight in Spain and forgotten her sunscreen. "Are you happy now?"

Daisy opened and closed her mouth. It was probably the first time anyone had rendered her speechless. I wanted to hate her for being on their side in the first place, but then I saw her eyes glisten and felt a bit sorry for her.

"I thought it was the right thing…" she said.

Kai raised his eyebrows. "Yeah, the right thing for *you*. You were just hoping you could make friends with all the rich Wishnook Vegas guests."

"That's not true!" she said and then stopped. "OK, it's a bit true. But I really did think it was the right thing for the town too. We can't survive without this development."

"Things have to change – I get it now. But we can't survive with Wishnook Vegas either," I replied. "Nobody can. You heard what they said."

She shook her head. "You're right. We're sunk either way."

Dad came over to us and took Mum's hand. I saw her fingers squeeze back. Then Declan came over and stood shoulder to shoulder with them. Mike the mechanic and Mr Percy looked at each other cautiously, then threw back their arms and hugged. One by one the whole town merged together, shoulders brushing, and I realised something had changed. They didn't want the Gold Rush money any more or the development. Not after what the suits had said about how they really felt.

"What's going to happen now?" asked Fabien.

I shook my head. The only thing I really knew was that now we were all in this together.

CHAPTER

TWENTY

It didn't take long for Mr James to send his decision, and for the diggers to roll into Wishnook. The judge hadn't heard the Gold Rush people's outburst, and even if he had, I don't think it would have changed his mind. Wishnook Vegas was going ahead. We'd lost the appeal.

"We'll lie down on the ground and refuse to move!" yelled Edna on the march up to the farm. She was on a mobility scooter and had taped a broom handle to the front, like a lance.

Daisy had her camera out again, but I didn't see the point.

The netting was back and beyond it were dozens of machines, trucks and cars. Gold Rush Properties weren't wasting any time. Wishnook was about to be obliterated.

Fabien dangled a pair of knitted handcuffs in front of everyone. "We can cuff ourselves to the diggers!"

"Great," I replied. "Let's just hope they don't have a pair of scissors or a thread unpicker."

Margot glanced up at the sky. "I could fly up and release water over them. I just need to find an air tanker and a captain first."

"Yeah, I'm not sure we've got time for that," Kai said.

The diggers were getting into position, ready to start.

I leapt over the gate and we all raced towards the diggers. It was the fastest I'd ever run and it really did feel like our lives depended on it. The digger engines buzzed fiercely, exhaust fumes filling the air. I choked on the smell and was suddenly aware of how small I was next to the huge beasts.

"What are you doing?!" yelled Jamie, the foreman. "You're trespassing on private property!"

"We're protesting!" I said.

I sat down in front of the diggers and prayed they wouldn't run me over. Kai did the same, and then the rest of the town caught up with us and sat down too. Fabien cuffed himself to a digger; then Mum uncuffed him and chained him to her instead.

Jamie tried to herd us all away, but the town dug their heels and bottoms into the grass. He puffed out his cheeks in frustration and went to call the police.

"How long will we have to stay here?" asked Fabien. "My sheep and goats will be wondering where I am."

"Maybe about thirty years," I said. "But I'm sure we'll get breaks."

It took three hours for the police to arrive from Windy Nook. While we waited, Farmer McAndrew set up a BBQ and started cooking Angus steak breakfast burritos. People took it in turns to unpeel themselves from the grass and smother their food in ketchup, before returning to eyeball the builders again. I was too worried to eat anything. All I could do was watch the birds overhead. They looked lost, landing on the hedges and then taking off again. One got its leg tangled in the nets, and I was terrified for its safety as the bird flapped its wings and eventually pulled itself to freedom.

A pair of police constables marched across the crunchy grass and tried to move us along, but nobody budged.

"I don't want to get arrested!" yelled Fabien, scrambling up.

"He wouldn't do well in prison," whispered Kai.

Margot grabbed hold of his hand and squeezed

it in reassurance. "Nobody's going to get arrested. Peaceful protesting is perfectly legal."

"It's perfectly annoying!" shouted Jamie.

"We're going to need more supplies," said Dad. "We might be here a while."

"I've got all those tents on the island, remember?" said Mum, and I thought back to when she'd run a wilderness yoga weekend, where the guests had slept under the stars. It had been a total disaster, mostly because our donkeys and goats kept breaking into the tents and licking the guests.

"We'll go back and get them, and grab some supplies while we're there," said Mum.

I didn't want to leave the protest, but there were too many tents for Mum and Dad to carry on their own.

Kai got up too. "Do any of your yoga guests have a computer?"

"I think one of them has a laptop. Why?" I said.

"I've got something to show you," he replied.

He wouldn't tell me what it was, even though I bugged him the whole way back. I ran from *Lady Agatha* to the house, where I found the yoga guests painting watercolours of Fabien's goats.

A posh guest was playing classical music on a laptop.

"Will you tell me what it is now?" I asked Kai.

He took a memory stick out of his pocket. "I dried out the SD card from my camera. Wanna see if the footage is still there?"

I stared at the tiny little card and felt disappointed. A few days ago I'd have been jumping with excitement. What good was watching our movie back now? The court case was over. Gold Rush Properties had won. It didn't matter who or what we'd recorded. It wouldn't make a difference now.

"There could be something on there that might help," said Kai. "It's worth a look, isn't it?"

I guessed it wouldn't hurt, but I didn't share his optimism.

The yoga guest put the SD card into his laptop and we all gathered round. Margot and Fabien sat cross-legged next to me on the grass. A folder opened, filled with files. Each one had a tiny squashed-up thumbnail of somebody we'd recorded. It looked like Kai had managed to save the SD card and the footage.

I opened the file and Declan filled the screen.

His gammon joint gleamed out at us, and he started talking about why he loved Wishnook, but then diverged into how he was a fourth-generation butcher and cured everything himself and made all the pie crusts by hand.

I sighed. Nothing here was going to help save Wishnook.

"I'd love to do a cooking course with him," said one of the yoga guests. "It's hard to find people this passionate about food these days. Does he run retreats as well?"

"Um … no…" I said, wondering why anybody would want to go on a retreat to learn how to make pies.

Next I played the footage of the offal. I wanted to die of embarrassment when Fabien came into the shot and stole the bucket. No wonder Daisy had used it in her movie. It made us look like lunatics.

"The mainland could really use a plant-based restaurant," mused another of the yoga guests.

"Exactly!" said Fabien.

"People around here don't like vegan stuff," said Kai, which made Fabien huff.

"You've not tried my seaweed paella," he said.

"It would attract more holidaymakers," said the yoga guest who was into his vegetables. "It would give people choice."

I wanted to give him a bit of a strange look, but maybe he was right. Daisy kept saying Wishnook was stuck in the past. Maybe there was room for a new restaurant in town. It would help Heidi's broccoli sales for one thing, and stop Fabien's protests.

The next thing I played was the footage of Dad's pootisserie. My embarrassment flooded back at the sight of the bizarre ornaments. There was no way anybody could think this was a good look for Wishnook.

"Oh, they're model cakes?" said a yoga lady. "We found some in the kitchen and thought they were balls for Wishnook cricket."

"What on earth is Wishnook cricket?" asked Dad, horrified. "They're pieces of fine art!"

"Oh, sorry," she said. "We've spent the morning whacking them about the island with mallets."

"Mallets?!" cried Dad.

"Don't worry, the balls are completely indestructible. That's why we thought they were for the game," she said.

Kai eyed her suspiciously. "Who told you about this game?"

"The chap who dropped us off at the island," she said.

Kai, Margot, Fabien and I all looked at each other. "Doug," we said at the same time.

It wasn't the first time Doug had made up stories for the yoga guests when he brought them to the island for us. Sometimes he told them the waters were infested with sharks, other times he'd make up customs, like having to greet everyone with a fist bump (resulting in Edna clipping one of them around the ear). As far as I knew, this was the first time he'd made up an entire sport.

The yoga guests got to their feet and gave us a demonstration of Wishnook cricket. It was a bit like normal cricket, only with mallets and wooden poos. Instead of stumps, they had to knock over a pyramid of tinned peas, and instead of running they had to do the floss down the central strip. It was the most ridiculous thing I'd seen, and I'd seen Fabien give a pedicure to a goat.

"It's the most fun we've ever had. We'd love to go and see a proper game of it. Is there an official league?" said one of the yoga guests, as they whacked a poo into the sky. They were quite right about them being indestructible.

"B-but … it's…" I stammered, not quite sure how to tell them Wishnook cricket was just a made-up game. I decided there wasn't much point in disappointing them.

Margot reached over me and played the next clip. It was of the netted hedgerows, the first time we'd seen them. The yoga guests all stopped playing cricket and gathered round the screen again. Their smiles turned to frowns and the laughter lines round their eyes disappeared. All I could hear were the waves in the background, sloshing back and forth.

The camera panned on to one of the little red birds, as it was freed from the netting. The oldest of the yoga guests sucked in his breath, and then yelled at us to pause the movie. I didn't blame him. It was too horrible to watch.

"Was that a red snicket?" he asked.

"What's a red snicket?" replied Margot.

"They're endangered," he said. "I'm a conservationist, and I've never seen one in Scotland before. In fact, I thought they were completely extinct in the UK. They're very particular about their nesting sites."

I zoomed in on the little bird, heart racing. The image was a bit blurry, but I could make out its little red wings and yellow beak. Now I thought about it I'd never seen one of those birds until I'd moved to Wishnook. In fact, I'd only ever seen them at the McAndrews' farm. They didn't even fly into town, let alone to our island.

What if they really were red snickets, though? The Gold Rush people were about to rip up their home! What if Wishnook was the last place in the country where they lived, and it was about to disappear? The thought made me feel sick.

"Where will they go, when the resort's built?" I asked. "Can we save them?"

"If they *are* red snickets, the resort can't go ahead," said the man. "The birds won't make a new home elsewhere. They'll keep going back to where their old one used to be, until they get injured or snatched by other animals. It would be a calamity for the species."

My heart began to race so hard I could actually hear it banging on my ribcage. "Do you mean Wishnook Vegas can be stopped?"

"If these birds are what I think they are, yes," he

said. "Their homes are protected. It will have to become a nature reserve for them."

Fabien leapt to his feet. "We're saved!"

"Well, I'm not completely sure these birds *are* red snickets yet," said the conservationist. "I'll have to verify it."

Margot leapt to her feet. "But the diggers are already at the field, ready to rip up the hedges!"

"Then there's no time to lose," the man replied.

I pulled him to his feet and together we all raced across the island, back towards *Lady Agatha*. A horrible feeling lodged itself in my tummy. What if we were too late?

CHAPTER

TWENTY-ONE

Lady Agatha thumped across the waves with a groan, and water bubbled up from a hole in the deck.

"Are we sinking again?" asked Fabien anxiously.

I grabbed the emergency tea set and began sloshing the water out. *Lady Agatha* gave one final groan and slowed to a sea-snail pace.

"Not now, Aggie!" I pleaded, giving the boat an encouraging pat.

Bang.

Smoke billowed from *Lady Agatha*'s engine and the mechanical buzzing sound cut out. A wave came up under us, and we rocked from side to side. Everything was quiet, apart from the sound of the water and the gulls.

"Not again!" cried Margot.

I turned to Kai. "What do we do?"

"See if you can fix the leak, and I'll look at the engine," he said.

Dad's eyebrows furrowed. "Maybe I should just call the coastguard."

"You do remember that the coastguard is Uncle Doug, don't you?" said Kai.

"Oh yes, good point," replied Dad. "Go ahead,

but please don't do anything to make the boat explode."

"If it does, it was going to happen either way," said Kai.

Fabien wrapped his arms round Margot's waist in fear. "Save me."

I couldn't believe this was happening now. The diggers were about to pull up the hedgerow and we were stuck in the middle of the sea. We were going to be too late, thanks to our useless old boat. We were so close to saving the birds and the town, but a million miles away too.

Mum knelt down to help with the leak, while Dad radioed for help anyway. I grabbed a pair of scissors from the emergency box, snipped a piece off my waterproof jacket and wedged it in the hole. It wasn't brilliant, but it seemed to slow the leak a little bit at least.

Kai whacked the engine with a spanner and it groaned into life again. "Step on it, before it breaks again!"

"I thought you were going to do something more tech than that," I said.

"First rule of when something breaks is to reboot it. Second rule is to hit it," replied Kai.

"They're not actually rules," said Margot. "And stay away from my aeroplane when I get one."

We crossed the sea agonisingly slowly, but I continued to bail out the water at lightning speed. My arms throbbed from the effort, but I was also glad to have something else to focus on other than the fact our town might already have been destroyed.

Finally we reached the harbour and I had never, ever been more grateful to see dry land. There wasn't time to cycle up to the farm, so Kai found the key to Doug's spare truck, and we motored along the road at the top speed limit. I closed my eyes, unable to look at whether the hedgerow was still there. At whether there was anything left to save.

"We're in time!" yelled Margot.

I opened my eyes. The hedgerow was still intact, and it looked like Jamie was still arguing with the locals. I jumped out of the car as soon as it stopped, and raced to the hedge to look for the little birds.

We tore at the nets, trying to find the red snickets. Behind us, the builders yelled threats and dialled the police again. I paused for a second and heard a rustling sound. The birds were still in the hedges; I could hear them.

"This is ridiculous!" yelled Jamie.

"If I'm right, you'll have to stop work immediately!" shouted the conservationist.

His hands were working over the netting much slower than mine, like he was searching for tiny pieces of gold. I guessed he didn't want to spook the poor birds. There had to be at least some stuck under the nets. I hoped the diggers hadn't scared all the others away from Wishnook.

"We've wasted enough time," said Jamie. "These hedges are coming down now."

"You can't do that!" I yelled.

"Watch me," he said.

He climbed into one of the diggers and turned on the engine. We ran after him, leaving the conservationist to search the hedgerows alone. We had to buy him enough time, even if that meant lying down in front of the digger.

We yelled at the rest of the town to make a circle round the machine. Dad had already explained everything about the birds to them and there was a weird feeling in the air, like a smoosh of fear and hope. I sat down in the mud and clutched

Margot's hand. Surely Jamie wouldn't run us over. Then again, I wouldn't put anything past the developers. We were all going to be worm food.

The digger moved forward. I pressed myself into the earth. I wasn't going to move. No one was going to harm the birds.

The digger inched closer. Doctor Ted, who was next to Fabien, screamed for his life and tried to make a run for it. Edna grabbed his ankles and rugby-tackled him back into position, as the digger made a beeline for the gap he'd left. Mum threw herself over Fabien, and Dad leapt up in front of them. A few people away, Heidi grabbed a rather unimpressive twig and brandished it at the digger.

"You shall not pass!" she yelled.

The digger got closer, closer, closer.

I shut my eyes and held my breath, hoping we weren't about to die.

Suddenly the engine noise stopped.

I opened my eyes a crack.

Jamie climbed out of the digger, his face red with annoyance. "You're all crazy," he said.

Everyone let out a huge sigh and then gave a cheer. Somehow we hadn't died.

I looked up in relief and saw a little red bird sweep across the sky.

"STOP!" yelled the conservationist.

"Is it...?" I began but felt too scared to ask.

There was a pause. It felt like an eternity.

"It's a red snicket. You can't build your resort here," said the conservationist.

"Are you sure?" I asked, hardly daring to believe it.

"Positive," he said.

My hands shook and tears misted over my eyes. Next to me, Fabien leapt into the air, almost as high as the birds. Mum started to cry happily too. The only person who looked annoyed was Jamie. He kicked his digger, then winced from the pain.

"It's the end of Wishnook Vegas!" I yelled.

CHAPTER

TWENTY-TWO

It was a few days later when my tummy started to churn. We might have stopped Wishnook Vegas, but how were we going to save the town? How were we going to make people come here now?

The birds were saved, but Wishnook wasn't.

I carried my worries to the next town meeting, where we all gathered inside The Wig and Pen. It seemed I wasn't the only one who was fretting about things.

"We could get one of those Michelin-starred chefs to work in your kitchen, Heidi," suggested Mum, when the mayor called for ideas on how to save the town.

Heidi nearly fell into a box of crisps. "Are you saying my food isn't fancy enough for the tourists? Because *I* can sell you a prawn on a lettuce leaf for seventy-two pounds."

"Could get an influencer to do a social media ad," suggested Brice.

"A who to do a what?" said Doug. "I swear I haven't understood a word you've said since the day you turned twelve."

"What about a competition?" asked Edna. "When Mr Billionaire gave away his island, the whole country was talking about Wishnook."

"Yeah, for all of two weeks," said Mike. "I'm sure they all googled us, but nobody actually came, did they?"

"We did!" yelled Fabien.

"Doesn't count – you're one of us now," said Mike, and Fabien's ears blushed with happiness.

This was ridiculous. None of us had any good ideas. But then I realised something. Something that I should have realised ages ago, but it had taken Margot's movie and mine to make me see it. I tried to organise the thoughts in my head, and an idea started to form. Maybe, just maybe, I knew what Wishnook needed to do.

I climbed on to the bar, ready to tell the town. This time I wasn't nervous about talking to them all. I didn't even have to picture them dressed up as donkeys.

The room fell silent and everyone's eyes focused on me. "My island and Wishnook are the weirdest places I know," I said.

"We're not weird!" yelled Jim.

Mrs Percy shushed him. "You've got a pet lobster and my husband sells ice cream on a wallpaper table. We're all barking mad, but in a good way."

"Yes, and that's my point," I said. "All the weird stuff is what makes Wishnook brilliant. It was the yoga guests who noticed first, when they were watching our movie. Instead of teasing Declan for serenading his gammon, they wanted to learn how to cook from him. And rather than thinking Doug's made-up game of Wishnook cricket was stupid, they thought it was the best game ever."

Doug snorted. "Sounds like they're the weird ones."

"We all are," I said. "Everyone in the entire world is a bit weird. But isn't that what makes it great? Isn't that what makes *Wishnook* great?"

"What's your point?" asked Daisy.

I glanced at Kai to help me out and he climbed up on the bar with me. "The point is, instead of trying to be perfect, we should show the world who we really are and what we have to offer. Declan could teach butchering and cooking lessons. Fabien could open up a vegan stall on the market. Mr Butterworth could organise a Wishnook cricket league. The McAndrews could run tours of their farm and tell people about barn safety. I could teach acting classes at the theatre, and The Rocking Pensioners could teach heavy metal songs to over-sixty-fives.

"Instead of hiding our weirdness from the world, we should show it off," I said. "We should show people that, yes, we're different, but that we're also fun, and if they come here, they'll never forget their holiday."

There was silence. I stared at the crowd, trying to work out what they were thinking. It was a long shot asking everyone to see our oddness as something good. Without the yoga guests maybe Kai and I wouldn't have seen it either.

"You're right, we are brilliant!" said Dad.

"Whenever people come here, we try to hide who we really are. Maybe we've been doing it wrong," said Heidi.

"So how do we tell the world about us?" asked Mike.

"We'll make one more movie," I said. "We'll hold a talent show, film it and make it into an advert for the town."

Everyone started chatting excitedly about how we were going to make the best movie ever. Mr Percy said it would be even more epic than *Titanic* but then Edna told him not to be ridiculous. I heard the McAndrews discussing their talents and Declan saying he'd been a professional competitive eater in his youth.

"I can do a dance routine with my goats!" said Fabien.

Mayor Oddway climbed on to the bar next to me and signalled for quiet. "OK, all those in favour of making a movie to show the world we're bonkers, raise your hand."

The entire town raised their hands.

Motion carried.

We were making another movie, and this time everyone was in on it.

CHAPTER

TWENTY-THREE

There were only a few hours until the talent show kicked off, but Fabien was still bent over his sewing machine, adding pleats to his cape. Margot sipped a cup of tea in her dressing gown and read the last page of a manual on how to fly a Spitfire. Meanwhile I just stared at Sunshine's old jumping rosettes and hoped she'd do well.

I made my way down to the beach and saw Mum stood in front of the yoga guests, saluting the sun with one hand and drinking a cup of strong-smelling coffee from the other.

Monty, Moon and Sunshine were waiting for breakfast by their stables. I stuffed hay into their feeders. They gobbled it up, and I tucked into my jam-covered toast beside them.

When Sunshine had finished, I walked her over to the edge of the beach and pointed out *Lady Agatha* to her. I'd spent the last two days following her around the island with buckets of sand, trying to desensitise her to it. Now it was showtime. I held my breath and prayed my plan had worked.

Sunshine lifted a hoof and tapped it warily on to the sand. I cheered, heart racing, and encouraged her forward with an apple. She took another step, then another and another. It was working!

I led her up a plank and on to *Lady Agatha*, which was just big enough to fit us all and a donkey. Sunshine wobbled uncertainly, her ears pinned back against her head. I stroked her neck soothingly, and plied her with more fruit and veg to make her feel better. Slowly her ears moved forward and I felt her relax.

Fabien danced his way across the beach with a group of goats following him. I tensed. It hadn't occurred to me that Fabien would need to transport his goats in Doug's boat too. There wasn't enough room for all of them. I shook my head at him, but Fabien flung a goat over the side of the boat regardless.

"You can't bring all these!" I said.

"Of course I can," he said, helping another goat scramble over the side. They were all on leads, with little coloured ribbons tied round their collars. They looked rather dashing, even though one was eating my flipflop.

Before I knew it, every inch of the boat was covered in goats, and a healthy smattering of goat poo too.

Margot, Mum, Dad and three yoga guests also

got in the boat, and stood pressed up against the stern.

"It's like Noah's ark in here," said Margot.

After a very smelly journey, we made it to the mainland. I'd expected to find everybody already in the theatre, waiting for the show to start, but instead they were all gathered at the little beach beside the harbour. I led Sunshine over to the shingly sand, into an enclosure that Kai had roped off for her. There were a series of jumps he and Doug had made out of scrap wood, and Sunshine bounded over them happily, ignoring everyone around her. At least she probably wouldn't eat these ones.

Before I could ask what was happening, Kai grabbed the microphone on a small karaoke machine he was holding and blew into the top of it. An excited hush fell over the town. I got out the camera and started to film, suddenly full of excitement. The talent show was starting!

"Welcome to the first Wishnook Talent Show," announced Kai. A Tom Jones song played in the background. He bashed the karaoke machine, trying to turn the backing music off, but it just got louder. The crowd laughed and Kai sat on the machine to muffle it.

"Sorry about this, I'll just have to talk over the music…" he said, getting off the machine, because his bottom was muffling his voice too. "Without further ado please welcome Daisy and her amazing surfing dog!"

My mouth fell open and I stared at Daisy. A surfing dog? That was ridiculous. I'd never even seen Daisy's dog anywhere near the water, and I'd certainly never seen it surf.

"How am I meant to compete with a surfing dog?" I muttered.

We all followed Daisy to the edge of the sea. There was a child-sized surfboard a metre up from the lapping waves. Pookie, Daisy's dog, leapt on it immediately, tail wagging. He yapped louder than Tom Jones.

Daisy pushed the surfboard into the water, past the breaking waves, until she was up to her neck in water. I watched Pookie anxiously, though he was smiling with his tongue out. Daisy looked around for a big wave, and silence fell over the crowd as we all waited in suspense.

"Surf's up!" boomed Kai's voice through the speaker.

A big swell made its way towards the beach. Daisy glanced over his shoulder, then pushed Pookie towards it on his surfboard. The wave came up behind him and the edge of it started to break. Pookie wagged his tail and barked at Daisy. She let go of his board, and Pookie caught the wave. It swept him towards the beach, and he ran in circles across the board, tilting it this way and that. The dog was surfing.

Pookie rode the wave all the way back to shore, and the crowd erupted into cheers.

"You've got to admit that was pretty impressive," said Margot.

I didn't want to admit anything, although it was hard to see how anyone else could beat that.

Kai checked the schedule Fabien had written for him and waved everyone towards the high street. "If you could all make your way to the theatre, we'll be treated to a sheep-shearing race by Mr and Mrs McAndrew!"

We all followed Kai up the high street, goats in tow, and into the theatre. Two sheep stood on the stage in a pen made from old fireguards. I wondered whether they'd be coming home with Fabien by the end of the show.

CHAPTER

TWENTY-FOUR

Kai climbed on to the stage, plugged the karaoke machine in and introduced the McAndrews to a song by the Backstreet Boys.

Mr and Mrs McAndrew chose a sheep each and stood over them holding pairs of automatic shears. Fabien tensed with excitement.

"Edna, please ready your stopwatch," said Kai.

On Kai's countdown Mr and Mrs McAndrew turned their shears on and plunged them into the sheep's coats. Clumps of wool flew into the air like snow and Fabien squealed with excitement. I tried to hold him back, but he shook me off, dived on to the stage and started gathering up armfuls of wool. His cloak whirled around him, like he was in a snow globe.

Mrs McAndrew finished shearing her sheep and dropped her shears in victory.

The crowd cheered and Fabien sneezed.

Mr Percy took to the stage next with his pet parrot. A German pop song blared out of the speaker and Mr Percy stood in front of his bird and started waving his arms around, like he was conducting a brass band. The parrot rustled its feathers, then opened its beak and started to sing.

"*Ich liebe dich*," the parrot crooned to the music.

Fabien shook his woolly head at me. "I don't believe it."

"I know. It's singing!" I said, open-mouthed.

"No, I mean it's the same song I'm doing my dance routine to!" he said.

I stared at him. "You're doing your dance routine to … this?"

"Yes," replied Fabien seriously. "I heard it in The Wig and Pen. It's perfect for the rise and fall of our routine."

"You know, sometimes I have absolutely no idea what you're talking about," I told him.

When Fabien had finished seething, it was his turn. As he rounded up his goats, I waited nervously, and when he disappeared behind the curtain the crowd muttered in confusion. Dad restarted the German song, and Mr Percy's parrot started singing again.

Just as the crowd were starting to get restless, Fabien burst through the curtains, his hand-sewn cloak billowing behind him. Sixteen goats followed. I knew there were sixteen because he'd knitted them little jackets with numbers on them.

Fabien started to dance, popping his elbows this way and that, and skidding across the stage in his trainers. The goats leapt around him in a surprisingly co-ordinated fashion. They bleated and he threw them treats from a pocket inside the lining of his cloak.

The whole crowd laughed with delight. I tried to follow his moves with the camera, but it was difficult because Fabien kept dipping up and down and swooshing this way and that. The crowd clapped along to the beat of the song, and Davy Jones the parrot continued to croon.

For his finale Fabien spun on his head, and his four eldest goats formed a pyramid in the background. They balanced on each other's backs like an overly hairy, bearded group of cheerleaders. Fabien winked at them encouragingly.

Eventually the German pop song ended. Again. Fabien did a celebratory spin on his head, then took a bow to rapturous applause. The goats deconstructed their pyramid and ran off together to eat the curtains.

None of the acts after that lived up to the spectacle of Fabien's dance troupe. Mum did a yoga demonstration with her guests, which was so boring Edna actually started snoring halfway through. The Rocking Pensioners sang a medley of rock songs with Frank's pet boa constrictor slithering round their necks. Dad live whittled another iced-bun poo, and Declan the butcher ate fourteen plates of potatoes during a competitive-eating contest with his cat (the cat only managed three plates and then slunk away with its hackles up).

I was so stunned by Wishnook's various and amazing talents that I'd completely forgotten about Kai's play. Just when I thought everything was winding down, he took to the stage and launched into a monologue about football and big dreams. I soon realised that he'd cast himself in the lead role (probably because he was the only person under seventy who was involved in the play), while Frank played his mother. It was the most bizzare thing I'd ever seen, with horrible acting and special effects that must have cost 30p from the joke shop in nearby Windy Nook.

Eventually the play ended and the cast linked hands and bowed. Nobody clapped. I saw Kai's crestfallen face, dropped the camera and clapped as loudly as I could. Fabien followed suit, and so did Margot. The clapping spread slowly through the crowd, until everyone was finally applauding.

Kai grabbed the microphone again. "Thank you, I hope you enjoyed it," he said, looking much happier. "Now, if you'd like to make your way outside, we have our two final acts!"

I looked around at everyone, trying to work out who hadn't gone yet, and then realised it was me and Margot. Now that the time had come to perform I felt a little bit sick. It was one thing being behind the camera but another to be directly in front of the lens. I hoped I wouldn't mess everything up and embarrass myself.

With a deep breath I headed back to the beach and got Sunshine ready. She'd been too busy eating and jumping to even notice I'd gone.

"You can do it, girl," I whispered as we approached the first jump, trying to reassure myself. "Just put one hoof in front of the other."

Sunshine flattened her ears back. I shushed her and wondered if she'd got stage fright. All I could hear was the lapping waves. Maybe the sand beneath us was freaking her out.

"It's OK. I believe in you, girl," I said soothingly.

Sunshine lumbered round the corner and her ears pricked forward. I held on tight and squeezed my eyes shut, too nervous to dare look. Suddenly I felt a rush of wind as Sunshine soared into the air. We landed with a bounce and I opened my eyes. We'd made it! We'd cleared the first jump perfectly.

I let out a whoop and patted Sunshine's neck. The crowd cheered as we sailed over the second jump. Sunshine turned on her back hoof and headed to the third jump. Things were going so well that I could practically feel the trophy in my hands.

"And here's Luna Butterworth, approaching the final hurdle," said Kai into the microphone.

Suddenly I heard a droning noise above us and I glanced up at the sky. A small plane soared just below the cloud cover. It was the same one Margot took her flying lessons in, but today it was pulling a banner.

"What does it say?" I heard Fabien yell.

Sunshine tossed her head at the sound of the plane and commotion.

"It looks like *Maggot loves Wishnook!*" came

a reply. "No, wait, that can't be right... *Margot loves Wishnook!*"

The plane lowered its nose and started to descend. My breath caught as Sunshine bolted away from the jump, dug in her hooves and rocked into a gallop. I clung to her neck as she picked up speed. My fingers gripped the reins and I tried to make a reassuring "shushing" sound, but it was no use. Margot's plane had terrified her.

"Luna, where are you going?" called Mum.

I was concentrating so hard on staying on that I couldn't answer her. Ahead, the makeshift fence Kai had constructed was coming up fast. We were going to crash straight through it!

CHAPTER

TWENTY-FIVE

I held tight with all my might and braced.

Sunshine leapt over the fence in one smooth movement and we soared out of the arena. The crowd scattered. Daisy's dog broke free and leapt on to its surfboard again.

Margot's plane banked away from us and Sunshine slowed to a calm trot. I glanced back at the scene behind. Mum had fallen in a pile of lobster pots and was trying desperately to free her foot from one, as a pair of claws snapped at her. Daisy's dog was halfway out to sea on his surfboard. Fabien had dropped all the sheep wool he'd collected from the shearing contest and now everyone was covered in varying degrees of fuzz.

It took a while to clear the carnage and for Margot to return from her voyage through the clouds. She strolled across the harbour in her aviator jacket and goggles, smiling from ear to ear.

"That was brilliant!" she beamed.

Pookie shook his damp fur on her feet, having finally been recovered from halfway across the Atlantic.

I decided to wait until later to yell at Margot for the noisiness of her plane, and instead looped my arm through hers. We gathered with Kai and Fabien to wait for Mayor Oddway to announce the show's winner. Somehow I doubted it was me.

He cleared his throat dramatically, but then Kai crept over to the karaoke machine and changed the backing track from Mozart to the *Bob the Builder* theme tune, and the crowd started to howl with laughter again.

"Oh, very funny," said Mayor Oddway. "As I was saying, the winner of Wishnook Talent Show is ... Fabien and his amazing goats."

Fabien jumped into the air and whooped. "I've won! I've won first prize at something! Can I go and tell the rest of my goats?"

Mayor Oddway hung a medal round his neck and Fabien's ears glowed pink with pride.

"Well done, Fabien," said Margot, lifting up his arm like he'd won a boxing match.

"The town's going to be OK now, isn't it?" I asked Kai.

He smiled. "I reckon so. I mean, we might not be Las Vegas, or even Wishnook Vegas, but we're still pretty cool. When people see who we really are, they'll come back."

"I think so too," I said.

"Let's go back to the island and borrow the yoga man's laptop again," said Margot. "We made a movie, and we've got a world to show it to."